D1355706

DRAYTON MANOR HIGH SCHOOL
ENGLISH DEPARTMENT

**HEINEMANN
NEW WINDMILLS**

## THE FLAWED GLASS

As a true islander Shona has always had a strong belief in the impossible and in magic. When her uncle leaves for America, the magic seems to fade but Shona cannot stop praying for the miracle that will unlock what is stored away in a body that can hardly walk and a tongue that can hardly speak. When Carl arrives on Shona's remote island the miracle does happen in the most unexpected way . . .

## ABOUT THE AUTHOR

Ian Strachan was born in Altrincham in 1938. At the age of twelve he acted on radio and at sixteen entered the theatre on the stage management side. He later went into television and has worked on productions of *Doctor Who* and *Z Cars*. As a child he read and loved thousands of books. He started writing for children because, he says, to a certain extent he felt he had a debt to repay. His first novel, *Moses Beech*, won the Young Observer/Rank Organisation Fiction prize.

Ian Strachan is now a BBC Radio Producer and lives with his wife and children in Staffordshire.

# The
# *FLAWED*
# *GLASS*

**IAN STRACHAN**

HEINEMANN
NEW WINDMILLS

Heinemann Educational Publishers
Halley Court, Jordan Hill, Oxford OX2 8EJ
a division of Reed Educational & Professional Publishing Ltd
MELBOURNE   AUCKLAND
FLORENCE   PRAGUE   MADRID   ATHENS
SINGAPORE   TOKYO   SAO PAULO
CHICAGO   PORTSMOUTH (NH)   MEXICO
IBADAN   GABORONE   JOHANNESBURG
KAMPALA   NAIROBI

ISBN 0 435 12368 8

Copyright © Ian Strachan 1989
First published by Methuen Children's Books 1989
First published in the New Windmill Series 1991

96 97 98 99 10 9 8 7 6 5 4

The moral rights of the author
have been asserted

Printed in England by Clays Ltd, St Ives plc

# One

Shona MacLeod sat at the back of the big, old classroom puzzling over the disappearance of the old magic. Until this last year it had coloured her life.

Miss Ferguson's voice droned on around the edges of Shona's thoughts like a bee round a jam jar. It was the last day of term and the long days of the summer holidays lay ahead. Usually that would have been the cause of great happiness and a sense of freedom to Shona, but not this year.

There seemed to be a great hole in her life. It was like a river bridge which two people, having started to build from either bank, had abandoned incomplete. Or a jigsaw, laid out on a table, from which somebody had now lost important pieces so that the body of the person in the picture is shown in detail but without a face.

She had felt the magic beginning to fade the day her Uncle James had left the island for America to seek his fortune, like one of the heroes from the old stories she so loved him telling her.

Shona remembered every word of those stories. Uncle James used to say that she was not taking in a word he was saying but it was not true, she could repeat them word for word. All those tales of seal-wives, mermaids and magic fish.

Every time he went out fishing in those last days she hoped that he would catch a magic fish, one that would grant him three wishes and make him rich so that he would not have to leave. But day after day he came back with perfectly ordinary herring. She feared that he had not recognised the magic fish and had thrown it back into the sea or that he simply was not trying.

At last the day came when he packed his bags, caught the ferry and went to the mainland to board a ship for America.

Shona knew he would never return.

She had tried to cling on to the magic by telling herself the old tales. But it was not the same. The magic grew fainter and fainter although she sensed she needed it now more than ever.

What she needed, she told herself, was a miracle. Not a small one, like her pocket money doubling itself, or an apple that replaced its flesh every time she bit into it, but a huge miracle.

What bothered her most was that a miracle would happen but she might not see it. It would be just like her stupid head to be looking in the wrong direction at the time and only catch a glimpse of it out of the corner of her eye. Like seeing the dying flash of a firework or the fading burst of a shooting star.

But she thought her miracle ought to be something noticeable, even if she was the *only* person to see it. Maybe one day a fully furnished house, complete with flush lavatory, would simply rise up out of a peatbog! That would be grand. Or would it? She loved their own little croft house just the way it was – given the choice the only thing she would change would be the horrid, old bucket lavatory down the yard which was guarded by millions of spiders.

Perhaps she ought to settle for the never-ending apple. But she waited for it to happen so often, after she had taken her first bite, that the flesh of her apples kept turning brown.

She just knew that she had reached a time in her life when something *had* to happen.

# Two

The huge, black, wooden door of the island's whitewashed school swung open with a bang. Children spilt out into the afternoon sunshine like corn from a slit sack. Running, shouting, laughing, fighting they tumbled towards the gate in the grey stone wall. Here they paused briefly to shout their goodbyes before splitting off into twos and threes to begin the walk home.

Shona MacLeod, as always, was the last to leave. Her thin pale hand gripped the blistered paintwork of the door frame whilst she summoned up the courage to negotiate the two narrow steps. She cocked her head slightly, as a bird might regard a worm, then shuffled her feet as she tried to organise her legs.

She leant her weight forward and made, as she did every day, a bad job of it. She slid off the top step, missed the second and almost fell forwards on to the gravel path, correcting herself only at the last second.

The worst part of the journey over, Shona heaved a sigh of relief and then, biting her lower lip as an aid to concentration, set off for the gate, swivel-kneed, her arms wildly flailing the air.

Miss Ferguson watched Shona from behind the orange curtain of the schoolroom window and gently shook her head. 'And what will happen to the child now, I wonder?' she whispered to herself.

When the summer holidays were over, four of her pupils, including Shona, would not return. They were old enough to go away to the big school on the Scottish mainland from which they would only come home for holidays or an occasional weekend if the winter gales allowed the boat to cross.

All well and good for the other three children, but what about Shona?

Miss Ferguson well remembered the young school inspector from the Education Authority who had come across to the island during Shona's first year at school.

He set tests for all the children. Most did the best they could, but after several attempts he was unable to get Shona to perform the simplest of them. Her grip was so uncertain she found it difficult enough to hold a pencil, let alone write letters or figures with it. And throughout she not only refused to utter the slightest sound, she would not look at him either.

Without being told she had guessed the importance of the man, who was only trying to help. Her response, to give as little away as possible, made her appear far less intelligent than she was.

During breaktime Miss Ferguson had seen him watching Shona standing in the shelter of the wall in the yard, silent and alone, whilst the other children played. When school ended for the day he had gone off to talk to Shona's mother armed with phrases like 'special needs'.

Mrs MacLeod would hear none of it. 'Who can look after her better than her own?' she demanded.

'But it would be in the child's own best interests,' he pointed out. 'After all, she wouldn't be alone. I hear her brothers already go to the mainland school. Besides the teachers there have special training for dealing with cases like this.'

Mr MacLeod, a short, tough man, who had been silently leaning against the mantelshelf, bit hard on his empty pipe. He would have been perfectly willing to let Shona go if only to give his wife a break from the constant attention Shona had needed from the day she was born. But the years had taught him that whilst he might run the croft and give orders

4

in a fishing boat it was unwise to interfere where Shona was concerned.

Mrs MacLeod's hands gripped together tightly in her lap. Her jaw set firm. 'A case, is she?'

The man, instantly regretting the tactless phrase, had the grace to blush. 'You know what I mean,' he mumbled.

She did. None more so. For who had cared for Shona all these years? Cleaned up her messes. Read her stories. Helped her with her first, clumsy steps. And all at a time when all the people on the island, including her own family, had secretly said, 'The poor child's nothing but a cabbage.'

The only person who gave her the slightest hope or encouragement was the man who had helped bring Shona into the world, old Dr MacGregor.

'Mrs MacLeod,' he had said, towering over her bed at the cottage hospital a couple of days after the baby was born, 'if she were a calf or a lamb we might well think of putting the poor wee thing out of her misery. But she's a person. One who will demand endless amounts of your time, energy and patience. Far more than any other child you are likely to meet.'

Dr MacGregor peered at her over his half-lens glasses and tugged at his beard. 'Life on a croft is hard enough, I know, and if you were to decide that this little babe is more than you can cope with nobody will blame you, least of all me. But if you decide to raise her, and you must fully understand what you are taking on, then I will give you all the help, support and knowledge I can. Though God knows I've seen few children with as bad a start as that poor wean!'

Mrs MacLeod looked at the thin, helpless little baby lying in the cot beside her bed. Its tiny arm was twitching helplessly. She guessed the little girl was trying to get her thumb into her mouth, to comfort herself.

For the first time since she'd seen the baby she leant over the cot. Very gently she helped the stick-like arm until the thumb was secure between the dribbling lips. Then the child gave a low moan of contentment.

Mrs MacLeod turned to Dr MacGregor. 'Her name is Shona and she stays with us, unless I fail her.'

And so she had. And through all the darkest times, when they thought that Shona was never going to respond, or to be anything more than a human vegetable, Dr MacGregor was there to help and encourage.

'Talk to her, Mrs MacLeod, talk to her!' he would urge.

'But I run out of things to say,' she had complained.

'Read her your shopping list, the advertisements off the back of cornflakes' packets or tell her stories from the Bible, anything, but *talk* to her or she'll fade, believe me!'

Then, one day, when she thought she would go mad from talking endlessly to a child who displayed no interest at all, she happened to turn and saw, for the very first time, Shona's eyes fixed on her and they were glowing. Having waited all those years for the slightest sign of recognition, let alone interest, surely she must be mistaken?

'Shona, do you like the story?' she had asked, though she felt foolish posing the question to a child who rarely even grunted and still could not move her head.

Not surprisingly there was no response. Disappointed she turned to continue with her work when, from behind her, she heard not one grunt but several following quickly and crossly upon each other. So she picked up where she had left off in the story. The grunts stopped, that glow came back into Shona's eyes and the faintest trace of a lop-sided smile appeared at one side of her mouth.

That was the first breakthrough.

'Aye, Doctor, but she'll never have the strength to move about, let alone walk,' Mrs MacLeod said one day when he had noticed not only a gain in weight but stronger pushes from the muscles in her puny arms and legs.

Dr MacGregor looked down at Mrs MacLeod in disgust. 'Then you'd best start saving up for a wheelchair.'

'No!' she protested.

'Then let us have no more talk of what she *cannot* do. I am beginning to think myself that with a little help she may yet surprise us all!'

'But walk?' Mrs MacLeod could not believe her own ears. Had the good doctor finally taken leave of his senses? 'How?'

Since the day Mrs MacLeod had named Shona, Dr MacGregor had, unknown to anyone else, been in touch with experts all over the world, trying to find the very latest knowledge of children who shared Shona's problems. 'There are certain exercises you might try her with,' he said.

Mrs MacLeod sat up, eager and ready. 'Yes?'

'They will maybe strengthen those muscles of hers, perhaps they will do no more than that. Strength is only part of the problem. Control is the other essential ingredient. One without the other would be useless, perhaps even dangerous. Imagine brute strength without the desire or ability to control it.'

'That is a risk we'll have to take. Show me the exercises,' she demanded.

The Doctor held up a hand to calm her down. 'They will mean hours of concentrated, hard physical work, on your part as well as Shona's.'

Mrs MacLeod would not take no for an answer. They began that very day. Hour after hour, week after week, with precious little to show for their efforts. It was the only time Mrs MacLeod saw Shona really cry. Having accepted all the deprivations of her life up to that point, one day the poor child was so exhausted by the demands her mother was making upon her that she wept in protest.

But slowly the muscles did begin to work. The head lifted a little and then the trunk. Her arms waved. Not to any purpose, but they did wave and with some strength in the gesture.

They reached the point where Shona could sit, at least for a while, and even stand, so long as her mother held both wrists. Mrs MacLeod said to the Doctor, 'Perhaps we should stop – maybe this is as far as we should go?'

'If you say so,' he replied calmly.

'We can't make her walk. It's too cruel!' she declared.

To her surprise he seemed to agree. 'You are right,' he

said with a brief nod, 'we can't *make* her. But I can't help wondering if it would be more cruel to deny her the chance of walking.'

Wearily, for the hundredth time since the child was born, she asked, 'How? How can I encourage her?'

'Move the things she wants, those she treasures most, a little further away,' he suggested. Even he had doubts about this idea. The last thing he wanted to do to this curiously contented child was to send her off into spasm of anger and frustration. Such treatment might well send even normal children into tantrums, if not hysterics. There was no knowing the effect it could have on Shona. He gave a shrug. 'You can but try.'

That the idea worked was more a testament to Shona's tolerance than anything else.

Mrs MacLeod knew more of Shona's problems and abilities than any young school inspector from the mainland. She had explored and faced up to them over many long weary years.

'There'll be time enough for the mainland when she's older,' Mrs MacLeod told the young man, and nothing he could say would alter her position. Shaking his head he left the croft.

So, every day Shona had gone to the island school. She had sat at the back of the class listening and watching intently but, so far as anyone could tell, unable to read or write. Indeed when she spoke, her own family could rarely understand her.

Only Shona knew that the words lay stored away in her head, neat and tidy as the clothes in her bedroom chest of drawers. It was just that when she opened her mouth to use them they flew out like clothes from the washing machine the day the door burst open in mid-spin. They all fell in damp, ugly piles, creased and spoilt.

Her lips, teeth and tongue would not obey her. Instead of words all she let out was a high-pitched wail and a thin trail of spittle which trickled down her chin. Sometimes her tongue seemed to grow too big for her mouth. The sounds were deep, dark grunts.

Writing her thoughts was out of the question. The marks she made could have been made by an animal for all the sense they made.

Her whole nervous system was a one-way street. Though she could hear, smell, see and feel like everyone else her body would not obey the commands she tried to give it. It felt to Shona like living a short way down a tunnel. She could see the escape route but could not achieve it. She was trapped for ever in her body.

Miss Ferguson had always been kind to Shona during her time at the island school. She included the child in everything the class did but she had always known she was failing the girl and now the law demanded that Shona must go to the mainland.

Miss Ferguson watched Shona, her long, red-gold hair tossed by the wind, until she disappeared from sight. She turned from the window and cleaned off the blackboard before locking up the school for the summer.

The golden eagle soared high above the island. His vast wings, equal in span to the height of a man, were supported by thermals as he inscribed lazy spirals against the crystal blue sky.

He ruled over the tiny island as his forebears once ruled over the whole country, until they were driven out by man's stupidity and poisons. But against all other creatures, both in the air and on the ground, he still reigned supreme.

And because of the height at which he flew he had a total view of his kingdom from the jagged cliffs in the East, where his mate guarded their eyrie, to the silver, Atlantic-washed, curved beaches of the West.

He watched the fishermen out in their boats trying their lobster pots, the crofters scything their hay and the tractor hauling a cart-load of rich, wet seaweed along the narrow road. He took in the high mountains, their shoulders peppered with white and purple heather, as easily as the lowlands where the hundreds of tiny lochans lay scattered like fragments of a smashed mirror, each reflecting the intense blue of the sky.

There is no peatbog, pocket-handkerchief-sized field, whitewashed croft, rabbit warren or mouse's nest which he does not know. This is his kingdom, his home and his larder.

He has heard whispers of the past borne by the winds. Speculation about the future he leaves to the restless minds of humans. His mind concentrated on the present and the hunger of the clutch of squealing young, perched high in their eyrie on the Black Mountain.

A young, juicy rabbit left the shadow of a rock. Enough tender meat to satisfy the pangs of his hungry brood.

Slowly he circled down. An unseen cloak of death falling silently across the sky. But there was a little girl with red-gold hair close to the rabbit. The rabbit sat up, twitched its nose in alarm then scuttled off, unaware of the greater danger it has escaped.

The eagle soared away, disappointed but still confident that his skill and knowledge will bring him other prey.

Shona stumbled across the machair, the tough, thin grass which is dotted with thousands of tiny pink and white flowers, towards the dunes and, beyond them, her favourite beach, its sand bleached silver by the sun. The wind tugged her hair, her body chilled beneath the pale green sweater and plaid skirt. She was tired and breathless but determined to reach the beach before she rested.

At last, she sank down in the sun-warmed sand, her back rested against the dune, her grey-green eyes stared out at the emerald sea.

Shona had always thought of this as her beach. Hers alone. Here her mind could escape the prison of her body and everything became possible. She could think herself into being a singer, an astronaut, gymnast, ballerina or any of the wonderful people she had heard about. She could explore, in her mind's eye, the dark twists and turns of a rabbit warren, swim to the bottom of the sea with silver, sharp-finned fish or fly like the terns that darted and twisted above her head.

Lying here she had re-told in her mind, hundreds of times, the stories Uncle James had told her while he worked mending nets or slicing out cubes of peat, neat and brown as tobacco. When the story, and the work, was done Uncle James would lift her high on his shoulders and carry her home whistling or singing as he went, no matter how hard the work had been.

Shona made up stories for herself about those rides. As she gripped handfuls of his curly, brown hair, perched high on his strong shoulders she convinced herself that she was riding along in a giant's ear, or that she was an Indian Princess, sitting in a golden howdah high up on an elephant's back.

'Shona!'

The voice was distant but Shona instantly recognised her mother calling her for tea.

Shona tried to call back. 'Hu-meen!' The right words would not come.

She put both hands down on the sand and pushed. It did not work. She rolled over on all fours like a dog and tried again. Shona hated the indignity of this. The only comfort was that on this occasion there was nobody to see her. She lurched up the dune.

'Shona! Are you coming?' Her mother's voice had grown impatient.

When Shona finally breasted the dune she saw her mother, a short but broad woman, standing in the doorway of their croft house. It was a four roomed, whitewashed, single storey cottage with a heavily thatched roof. Shona thought the bright sun shining on the whitewash made the house glow with a special warmth.

The second her mother was certain Shona was coming she turned and went back inside. The truth was that Mrs MacLeod avoided watching Shona walk when she was coming towards her because she didn't want Shona ever to see the pity she could not keep off her face.

11

It was part of the guilt her mother had carried with her from the day Shona was born. She had always, though quite without reason, felt guilty about Shona. She blamed herself that this child, who had come from her body, was not perfect. The guilt was one reason why she had so readily accepted Dr MacGregor's challenge.

As her mother turned away Shona sighed. Whenever her mother did this a loneliness came over her, as if in some way she was being shut out. The trouble was that everything she did took her too long and nobody, not even her mother, had the patience to wait.

Perched high in their eyrie the female golden eagle was busy with her vicious beak, disembowelling the small otter the male had brought back. Clutching it with her talons, hacking at it with the hook of her beak, she offered the bloody morsels to her young. Greedily they gobbled them down. Each day it grew a little more difficult to satisfy their hunger. Soon they would fight over the largest pieces. Maybe only the strongest of the three would survive. The others might not live long enough to fly. Eventually both parents could gather food but it still might not feed three eaglets.

Usually she only laid one egg, sometimes two and this is the first year she has ever hatched three. She still remembered the pride at seeing the three eggs, 80mm long, white blotched with reddish-brown.

During the six long weeks she sat on them she wondered about the third egg. Two hatched almost together. She began to grow nervous and wonder if the third was addled. She was on the point of abandoning it, tipping it out of the nest, when she heard faint sounds of chipping coming from inside the shell. She knew she must not help. If it was not strong enough to break the shell it would not survive anyway.

The tapping grew fainter and fainter and then stopped altogether. She thought it had given up the struggle but then it began again, stronger and louder, and at last the first hole

12

and a tiny, hooked point of a beak appeared through the shell. It rested again for a short while but then, encouraged by the sounds of the other chicks, it set to work until the shell was shattered and the blind, bald chick emerged.

As she fed them the last scraps of otter she could not help wondering if that was the one which in the end would not survive. Even though they had all three grown bigger and were covered in white down she could still easily tell them apart. The last to emerge was the smallest. Maybe its original struggle for life was all for nothing.

She gazed out towards the eastern horizon where she could just make out the mainland. The car ferry, with its two squat red and black funnels, set either side of the white superstructure above the black hull, was just setting out towards the island on its regular nightly visit.

Nobody on the island knew how much its arrival would affect all their lives.

# Three

A boy, deeply tanned, with intense blue eyes behind large-lensed glasses, his long blond hair slicked back by the wind, was perched on the bow rail of the ferry. Whilst one hand held the rail the other pointed ahead excitedly. 'Mom, I can see the island!'

His mother, whom he resembled except in height, huddled down inside her vivid, yellow quilted anorak and used the deck house as a shelter from the cool sea breeze.

She nudged her husband. 'Howard, he's going to fall overboard and drown before we ever get to your beloved island,' she drawled in an American accent that had the warmth of the south in it.

Howard eased the panatella from between his thick lips. His accent was harsher, more Chicago, but the cut of his clothes suggested Manhattan. 'Carl! Get down off that rail.' Carl instantly obeyed, he always did. Sometimes his father wished he wouldn't, that he had more guts. Though he loved his son, the boy was too pliable for the taste of a man who had founded a financial empire on the wrecking trade.

Carl was still pointing. 'Can't you see it?'

His father nodded, he'd clamped the cigar back between his lips, but it was easy to see, from the slow grin round the corners of his mouth and the light in his eyes, that he was as excited as his son. He thrust his hands deep into his trouser pockets and rattled the unfamiliar British coins.

Beverly Kleinberger was not only cold but tired. It had been a long journey. Breakfast in their London hotel suite now seemed to have been eaten in the previous week rather than earlier that same day. An early flight from London to Glasgow, the slow train journey up the West Coast of Scotland only to discover the ferry was an hour late. Locals, used to the ways of the sea, accepted it as common practice. Tourists, particularly Americans, regarded it as yet another example of British inefficiency.

The reddening sunset turned the waves to pewter. Peering into the rays they could just make out the jagged outline of some rocks rearing up out of the sea ahead. In silhouette they reminded Carl of a dinosaur's back. His mother's only thought was of a shipwreck; she shivered.

Howard sighed with contentment. 'How about that, Bev?' As he spoke the red end of his cigar zapped about in the dark like a firefly. 'Hey, Donna's missing all the fun. Shouldn't we wake her yet?'

Beverly hurriedly shook her head. 'She's bushed, let her sleep as long as she can. She'll be cranky enough when she wakes.'

Despite it only being a two-hour crossing they had booked the State cabin, much to the amusement of the other passengers. The Kleinbergers were used to travelling in style especially Carl's younger sister, Donna. It would have been more to her taste to have done the trip in her father's personal Leah jet. An idea which had been prevented from becoming reality not only by the lack of an airstrip on the island but mainly because of her father's romantic notion of arriving at his newly acquired island by water.

'You don't get to be a Laird every day of the week,' he had grinned when he first told them about the trip to their new home, 'and I want to do it right.'

Behind his back Donna had been scornful. 'Who does he think he is – Bonnie Prince Charlie?' The very last place she wanted to spend the summer was a remote island somewhere off the coast of Scotland. A condominium on the Florida coast or a beach house at Malibu would have been more her style.

*

More islanders than usual had gathered on the grey, stone quay to meet the ferry and an expectant buzz ran through them knowing that it was bringing the island's new owner. Several islanders, over on the mainland for a visit, had spotted the American family waiting impatiently for the ferry and had instantly phoned home, regardless of expense! Those with telephones had been quick to spread the word to those without and also knew the ferry was running an hour late and had not wasted time by getting there too early.

A new Laird was not a rare event. Since the end of the war in 1945 the island had been bought and sold as frequently, and as casually, as a pound of tea. Previous owners had included a merchant bank, an Arab sheik and an insurance company. Some of the owners had paid brief visits. Usually they came around the Glorious Twelfth for the shooting, or in early summer to take brown or sea trout from the lochs. But none had stayed for more than a fortnight or returned for a second visit, preferring to remain absentee landlords free to dispose of this 'unusual, remote and attractive property' when land prices rose to give them sufficient profit from their speculation.

The difference this time, the islanders had been astonished to discover, was that the latest owner, a rich American, was not merely visiting but intended to come and live in the Big House, at least for the summer.

In the past Mr MacPherson, the Factor, whose job it was to run the island, had collected rents, agreed to minor repairs and received his instructions from the owners by phone or post. Neither MacPherson, nor the islanders, knew how they would fare with a resident Laird looking over their shoulders.

Fishing, farming (including the experimental bulb and deer farms), the collection of seaweed, the shops and hotel, even the weaving sheds which produced the island's tweed, all depended for their existence on the whim of the Laird. Day by day decisions had all been taken by the Factor. Few of the businesses made more than marginal profits, the

16

property rents were controlled and their repairs expensive, consequently the landlords were not interested in anything but speculative land values.

Mr MacPherson was an incomer, not an islander, and though a little formal he was fair and, most important of all, he always tried to keep the island's, as well as the islanders', best interests at heart during his dealings with the landlords. Often he had decided not to 'bother' the Laird over a particular problem, especially if he thought he might get the wrong answer!

A Laird in permanent residence for the first time in living memory would make life very different. The Laird owned the whole island and everything on it. There wasn't a man, woman, or child whose future did not depend on him. It was no wonder they were anxious for their first sight of him.

Shona was not on the quay. She hated crowds and particularly visitors who, she thought, were apt to stare at her. She had a favourite grassy knoll which overlooked the floodlit quay from which she could see everything.

Shona too had heard of this new man coming from America and she could not help wondering if the Laird was in some way connected with her Uncle James. Perhaps they had met out there. Uncle James might have told him what a wonderful place the island was and the American had been so impressed he had rushed out and bought it the very next day!

Shona sighed. More fanciful imaginings. She knew her idea was stupid. America was a huge country full of millions of people. But suppose they had met and the American had brought a message for her from Uncle James? Perhaps she should have been down on the quay after all!

It was too late. The ferry was docking. Thin ropes snaked out from the side of the ship. They were caught by men on the quayside who hauled on them to bring fat, black hawsers out of the sea which they looped over the bollards.

Shona watched the ferry's huge white doors open. It made her think of a great whale opening its mouth to disgorge the contents of its stomach. Tourists' cars toiled up the ramp in a cloud of grey-blue exhaust fumes. The instant they touched dry land they set off in a burst of confidence which evaporated the moment they realised it was dark, there were no streetlights and they did not know where to go. Their dismay increased when they asked the locals but could not understand a word of the helpful directions because their ears were not yet tuned to the accent.

But tonight Shona and the rest of the islanders barely glanced at the tourists. Even the hotelier, Hamish MacDonald, swiftly rounded up his flock of weary guests like a sheepdog, corralled them without ceremony in his mini-bus, then returned to watch. Groceries piled up unnoticed beside Mr MacKay's van and the vital car parts for the garage mechanic, Mr MacBratney, lay unheeded beside him.

Even Fergus, the postman, in his usual uniform of regulation jacket and hat worn with waders, seemed remarkably uninterested in what he referred to as 'the Mails'.


Beverly glanced nervously down the gangway at the silent ring of dark islanders waiting on the quay. There was no sign of a Welcome Wagon! 'Are they going to lynch us?' she whispered to her husband. She felt Donna's grip on her hand tighten.

'Don't be silly!' Howard hissed out of the corner of his mouth.

Carl stood silent beside his father thinking it was like watching a scene from an old, black and white movie on 'The Late Late Show'. Bogart arrives in Shanghai!

Bev wondered, 'Do they expect you to make a speech?'

'If they do, they'll be disappointed.'

As they reached the quay a tall, thin man dressed in brown tweed plus-fours, who looked to Bev as if he was auditioning for 'Brigadoon', stepped forward from the group and extended his hand. 'Mr and Mrs Kleinberger? I'm your Factor, MacPherson, we spoke on the telephone.'

Howard let out an audible sigh of relief that the silence had been broken. He grabbed MacPherson's hand and pumped it harder than was necessary. 'Hi! Good to see you. This is my wife Beverly and my children Donna and Carl.'

MacPherson nodded politely to them. 'I'm sure your journey must have been trying . . .'

'You can say that again,' murmured Bev.

'. . . I have the car waiting to take you up to the house.'

'Lead on, MacDuff!' Howard grinned. The grin faded when he saw the reaction of MacPherson who turned abruptly on his heel and headed for the white Range Rover without a word.

From the moment the Americans had stepped on to the quay Shona had been unable to take her eyes off them. Their clothing alone, vivid splashes of pink, yellow and green, was enough to make them stand out amongst the islanders dressed in subdued browns, blues and greens which blended more easily with their surroundings. It was as if a species of rare and exotic migratory birds had been blown off course and had suddenly arrived amongst the island's crows, geese and ducks. The man wore a blue baseball cap but the blonde hair of the mother and of her two children shone under the floodlights like pale, gold threads.

The daughter, Shona thought, was about her own age, though her sophisticated hairstyle, shoes with a slight heel and a hint of make-up made her seem older.

But it was the boy, who was about the same age as her brothers though slighter in build, who really captured Shona's attention. She did not notice he wore glasses, could not have said what he carried but there was an aura about him which she found hypnotic and when he climbed into the Range Rover with his family and drove off it was as if the floodlights over the quay had been switched off.

By the time she had stumbled home, thinking about the American boy every step of the way, the first hint of golden daylight had appeared in the eastern sky, so short are summer nights so far north.

From the Range Rover Carl could see the Big House lived up to its name. It was a stone built house on three floors with high, rectangular windows and white stucco pillars which supported a mock-classical portico above a huge panelled front door.

They all thought it looked rather grand until they got closer. Then, even by the headlights, tired as they were, they noticed weeds poking up through the sparsely-gravelled drive, white paint flaking off the window frames and the web of cracks which riddled the stucco on the pillars.

What had finally taken the frosting off their cake was when MacPherson was unable to unlock the rather grand front door, despite the huge iron key he used.

'The lock seems to have seized up with rust,' he apologised. 'I'm afraid we'll have to use the kitchen door, that's never locked.'

Bev and Howard looked at each other in amazement. Their unspoken thought was that if they had done that in New York they would have returned to find the place stripped down to the light fittings.

As they made their way through the cavernous kitchen, lit by a low-powered bulb, with its old-fashioned white sink, scrubbed pine table, huge grey enamel electric cooker and worn, flagged stone floor, Bev muttered under her breath, 'You can see why nobody would want to steal anything!'

Howard silenced her with a dig in the ribs.

Once in the oak-panelled hall MacPherson gave them the briefest of explanations as to where everything was – nobody felt they could face a grand tour, bade them goodnight and left. Everybody was exhausted. The journey across the hall, up the broad staircase with its threadbare carpet and across the landing to their rooms seemed like a route march. Their only thought was to shut their doors and crash out on the beds which thankfully Flora, who had been engaged as a cook-housekeeper, had made up and aired ready for them.

They had chosen the rooms and found their way to them

with the aid of plans of the house which the efficient MacPherson had sent.

Carl liked his room on sight. The heavy, dark furniture was a total contrast to his hi-tech, metal and plastic, room back home but he found the old, used air it gave off quite friendly. It felt like slipping back into a coat he had not worn for some time. He explored the massive, mahogany wardrobe, built like a small castle, and was amazed when water actually ran out of the brass taps over his basin. He unpacked his overnight bag. The bulk of their luggage was following them.

Having got quite drowsy from the heat of the car during the journey he was now surprised at how awake he felt. He drew back the dusty, old curtains with a clatter of wooden rings along the pole. It was daylight! Having so recently seen the sunset he thought he must be dreaming or that he had lost all sense of time.

While he cleaned his teeth he gazed out of the window at the vista of the grass, sand dunes and beyond them the sea, revelling in the sense of space and freedom. His room was on the back of the house facing west.

Donna thought her room smelled of moth-balls. She found the walls dark and oppressive. The heavy, brown curtains, the worn, Wilton carpet and the red, paisley-patterned bed cover were dull and shabby. Donna was used to brand new things in fashion colours which she was happy to change, much to her father's annoyance, twice a year if need be.

Above all she hated using other people's belongings. To her this whole house had a feeling of being second-hand, well-used by people she did not care to think about too deeply, in case thinking about them caused them to appear before her.

It felt to Donna that the room was trying to swallow her up. This was partly because there were, apart from her pink overnight bag, none of her own possessions in it and too many of other people's. She felt in danger of being so overwhelmed she would become a non-person, lose her identity completely.

Hastily she undressed and climbed into bed, knowing that she was not going to sleep because she was too busy trying not to think about all the people who had lain there before her. Some of whose portraits she had tried to avoid looking at on the stairs.

She neither knew nor cared which way her room faced, she simply wanted to be back in *her* bed, in *her* room in New York.

Howard and Beverly had the master bedroom at the front of the house which faced east, directly into the morning sun.

Lying in the vast bed and gazing round the room he said with a yawn, 'The whole of my mother's flat in Chicago would drop into this room without touching the sides.'

Beverly was drifting off to sleep wondering what the rather unusual smell was coming from the pillowcase, until she realised it was fresh air.

'Keee-ya!' The loud cry came from outside the window.

Beverly sat bolt upright, with Howard's arm in a grip like a vice. 'What was that?'

'Hmmm?'

'Something screamed outside the window. There's a wild animal out there.'

Howard opened one, pink-rimmed, eye. 'An animal – outside a second storey window?'

'Keee-ya.'

'There it is again. Go see what it is, Howard.' As he threw back the bedclothes Bev grabbed his arm again. 'No, don't leave me!'

'Bev! Make up your mind. Do you want me to take a look or not? I'm tired, I want to get some sleep.'

Reluctantly she released her grip. 'All right. But take care.'

Howard climbed out of bed shivering. 'It's freezing out here!' When he reached the window he threw back the threadbare curtains and blinked in the daylight which flooded the room, hurting his eyes.

Bev, crouched in bed with the sheets pulled over her head for protection, whispered, 'What is it, Howard?'

'Keee-ya,' it went again.

'How do you like that?' Howard laughed.

'What is it?'

'A seagull. It's sitting on the stone balustrade just outside the window.'

'Well, get rid of it, Howard! I can't sleep with that racket going on.'

'How?'

'Flap your arms or something, I don't know. Do whatever it is you have to do to get rid of seagulls.

Howard flapped his red pyjama'd arms. The seagull flapped its wings, by way of reply, just enough to lift it a foot off the balustrade. Then, seeing the threat was more imaginary than real, it dropped down again. 'Hey! Will you look at that?'

Bev, already tired, was getting testy. 'Howard, I don't want to look at it, I *want* to go to sleep. Get rid of it, please, and come back to bed!'

Howard flapped his arms, more vigorously than before but the seagull merely rose an extra couple of centimetres in the air and then settled again. He banged on the window.

'Keee-ya! Keee-ya!'

He banged harder and shouted at the bird. 'Go away! We don't need you! Get the hell out of here!'

'Keee-ya. Keee-ya. Keeee-ya!'

'Howard!' Bev banged her fists on the bed. 'I asked you to get rid of the damned bird, not do a duet with it!'

The door opened and Donna, her blonde hair tousled, wearing a pink nightshirt with a picture of Snoopy on the front, wandered into the room. 'What's all the noise?'

Howard was not pleased to see her. 'That's really great!'

'Your father is trying to get rid of a seagull from outside our bedroom window so that we can all get some rest.'

Exasperated, but determined to succeed, Howard pushed up the heavy sash window and bellowed at the bird, which was already airborne. 'Clear off! And don't come back!'

Beverly, her teeth chattering, wailed, 'Close the window for goodness sake, it's freezing in here.'

'You wanted me to get rid of the seagull, didn't you?' he said as he slammed the window down.

Carl, still fully dressed, poked his head round the door. 'What's all the racket?'

Howard threw his hands in the air. 'Great! Now everybody's awake. Let's have a party! Doesn't anybody want some sleep around here?'

Beverly explained. 'Your father was getting rid of a seagull, that's all. It's gone now, so you can all go back to bed.'

'I'm never going to sleep in my spooky room,' Donna whined.

'Leave the curtains open,' suggested Carl, 'I have.'

'But look at it!' Donna pointed at the daylight streaming through the window. 'It's broad daylight . . .' she broke off to look at her pink Swatch and could not believe what she saw. 'At two o'clock in the morning? I could have sworn I set my watch right when we landed at Heathrow.'

'It's right, honey,' Howard assured her. 'This far north there's hardly any darkness in the middle of the year. In the winter it's daylight they're short of.'

'Children!' Beverly interrupted before the geography lesson got out of hand. 'Let's all go to bed and try to get some sleep. Come on, now!'

When the children had left and Howard had closed the curtains and got back into bed Beverly closed her eyes. Peace reigned and she felt herself starting to drift off again.

'Keee-ya.'

'Oh, no!' moaned Beverly.

From outside the window, in a slightly lower tone, there was another, 'Keee-ya.'

Howard murmured, 'I think he went away to find a friend.'

# Four

The islanders copied the birds and animals by rising early. They used the long daylight hours they were given in the summer not only to get through their daily tasks but to start making preparations for the short, bleak days of winter.

Shona woke early but she did not get up. She had lain in her bed for hours looking at her green curtains and how the sunlight made the pattern of flowers look real enough to pick.

Lying there reminded her of the days when she was tiny, before her muscles were strong enough to allow her to turn her head. Never having known any other way of life she would lie for hours, never crying, waiting for her mother to come to her. Sometimes she would hear her mother in the room with her but be unable to turn to see her. Still she did not cry.

'She may have missed out on some things when she was born,' her mother used to say, 'but she's got enough patience for all of us!'

Shona knew she was no more patient than anyone else. It was merely that she was saving her anger, frustration and determination for things which *really* mattered, like learning to do things for herself and, particularly, how to walk. Without which she would remain a prisoner.

As Shona lay in bed the image of the blond-haired boy at the Big House kept whirling round in her head but somehow it had got tangled up with something else.

Amongst the stories Uncle James had told her were

several about princesses. There was one particular princess who had meant more to Shona than any other.

When the King and Queen realised their beautiful baby daughter was in mortal danger a trusted servant had spirited her out of the castle and given her to a fisherman and his wife to look after until it was safe for her to return to the palace. As she grew older the fisherman told her the true story of her birth and though she was very happy with the poor fisherfolk she waited anxiously for her parents to come and collect her.

One day they heard that her parents, the King and Queen, had been murdered, a cruel tyrant had claimed the throne and so it was unlikely that anyone would come, apart from somebody who intended her harm, for now she was the rightful heir to the throne. The little princess was very unhappy. She cried and cried but she realised she would have to make the best of it and made herself useful by learning how to mend nets and cook fish. But, though her foster parents were very kind, it was a hard life, and she secretly longed to return to the palace, though that seemed impossible now.

But it so happened one day that the fisherman was out in his boat when the sky blackened and a terrible storm blew up. Making for home he came across the wreckage of a sailing ship which had but one survivor: a boy, whom the fisherman rescued and took home with him to recover from his ordeal. As soon as he set eyes on the beautiful girl who nursed him the boy fell in love with her and, although he took her to be the fisherman's daughter, he asked her to marry him. She agreed. Only then did he reveal that he was really a prince of noble birth but imagine his surprise when she told him that she was a princess.

Shona had often wondered if there was some secret about her that her parents had not told her. Maybe she was really a princess but her true parents had been so ashamed of her when she was born that they had given her away. Not that she didn't love the people she *believed* to be her parents but she could not help wondering if a prince was ever going to come and rescue her!

What kept buzzing round her brain was this curious mixture of the new Laird's son and the princess who needed rescuing.

'If anybody ever needed rescuing,' Shona thought, 'it's me!'

Her mother's voice from the living room interrupted her daydreams. 'Are you ever getting up today?'

Being unused to daylight and seagulls in the small hours everyone at the Big House had slept badly except for Carl. Consequently he was the only one who, instead of lying in bed suffering, had decided to get up, put on a thick sweater and explore his new home.

He started in the kitchen mainly for the very practical reason that he was very hungry. When he went through the previous night although he had not noticed an ice-box he had noticed two other big, oak doors apart from the one by which they had come in and the other that led to the main part of the house. The word 'pantry' had stuck in Carl's mind, probably from reading *Mary Poppins*, and he was convinced that that was where one of the other doors would lead.

He was right. But most of the food needed cooking before it could be eaten, sides of ham, some strange-looking sausages and eggs. He pulled the top half off a crusty cottage loaf and ate it with a lump of hard, yellow cheese.

His hunger temporarily satisfied Carl tried the other door. Stone steps led down into a dark cellar. He had never been in a cellar before in his life. He found a light switch and went down.

The cellar was vast and seemed to go under the whole house but, having been brought up on re-runs of *The Munsters* and *Dracula* he found them very disappointing. The only interesting discovery was a rack of bottles of wine so thickly covered in dust they seemed to be wearing woollen jackets. Dad would like to know about those! But apart from the wine and several million spiders it was very dull and Carl thought he would have better luck outside.

From his bedroom window he had noticed a range of outbuildings.

Carl went back up the steps, pushed open the door and a woman's scream almost made him fall back down again.

'Mother of Mercy! You've taken the life out of my body and the breath from my lungs.'

A fat, red-faced woman, dressed in black, sat in a chair, her legs splayed out, fanning herself with her hand.

'Hi! Are you Flora?' Carl asked.

'I am. And I'm here to cook meals and look after the house, not to have my life shortened by shocks like that one. I thought you were the Devil himself coming straight up from Hell!'

'I'm not the Devil, Flora, I'm Carl.'

'Will I know the difference?'

Carl grinned. 'Mostly, I guess. The one you need to watch out for is my kid sister, Donna.'

'It'll be your parents I'll need to watch out for if I'm late with the break fast on your first day with us! Make room now, I've work to do, Master Carl.'

Carl made his way across the courtyard turning over in his mind not only her soft, lilting voice but her choice of words. The way she had split 'breakfast' into two words and the fact that she had called him 'Master Carl'!

The outbuildings were built of the same stone as the house and formed three sides of a square round the yard. There was stabling for three horses and an old cowshed but no sign that either had been used for their proper purpose for years, just dusty garden implements, mouse-eaten hessian sacks and a heavy, wooden wheelbarrow with a broken wheel.

The third and far more imposing building was the coach house with its tall wooden doors and a little white tower on top which housed a clock. The black hands of the clock pointed permanently at half-past six, as if, tired of travelling round the face, they had dropped to that position from exhaustion.

He tugged back the wooden doors. Inside was a curious little carriage which had once presumably been drawn by the long departed horses. Its green leather seats were cracked and faded with tufts of horsehair poking out.

Carl was enjoying his exploration and he was on his way across the courtyard towards a wrought iron gate in the wall, which led into some sort of overgrown garden, when his father called down from an upstairs window.

'How're you doin'?'

'Fine, Dad. I think I'm going to like it here.'

'Me too. Come up to the house for breakfast.'

'Break fast, Dad,' Carl said, quoting Flora.

'What?'

'Never mind.'

By the time Shona was dressed in holiday clothes her parents had long since finished breakfast. Her father, having milked their house-cow Morag, had gone out fishing for herring in the boat he used to share with Uncle James.

Shona's mother was brushing up ash in the broad hearth. 'I don't want you under my feet all day, young Shona,' she declared. 'Your brothers are due back from school on tonight's ferry and I've enough to do.'

Her mother often sounded sharp but Shona knew she was probably the kindest person on earth. Shona nodded and smiled as she poured some of Morag's creamy milk over her porridge.

'Easy with that milk now! We've barely enough for the day.' She shook her head. 'I reckon old Morag's for the long walk before too long.'

The 'long walk' meant the two mile hike to the animal auction known as Fair Day which, every summer, took place at the south end of the island. Because there were no cattle-wagons on the island the livestock was all driven to the sale on foot.

Shona loved the shaggy, dun-coloured cow who had given them milk for as long as she could remember. She remembered squatting in a corner of the little stone byre, with the winter winds howling outside, watching her father draw streams of milk into the bucket he clasped between his knees. It was unthinkable that Morag should be sold to anyone else. It would be just like selling a member of the family.

'It's no good pulling a long face,' her mother said. 'There's no use in a house-cow that eats us out of house and home and then gives nothing in return. We'd be better off buying the milk. You'll be wanting us to buy woolly jumpers for the sheep next!'

Shona had to smile. She knew her mother was right so she did not argue. Shona rarely tried to speak even to her mother, most of what she wanted to say could be got across by facial expressions or gestures.

'Make haste and be off into the good fresh air,' her mother urged the second Shona put down her porridge spoon.

One of the sorrows, for both of them, was that Shona was no help around the house. It was quicker for her over-worked mother to do the job herself rather than stand anxiously waiting for something to be dropped while Shona dithered. They rarely enjoyed the experience of working together and Shona never had the satisfaction of a job well done.

But today she needed no second bidding.

It was a glorious day. The corncrakes were 'arp, arping', hidden by the long grass near the fence.

At the beach the tide was out. Black and white oyster-catchers were warbling their high-pitched trill as they picked over the stranded seaweed for small insects and sea creatures.

The temptation to lie in a sand-dune and daydream all day, was enormous but Shona resisted it. From the moment she had got up her sole intention was to go up to the Big House where she might get another glimpse of the new boy.

Except for Carl, who had gulped down a bowl of porridge and gone out again, breakfast at the Big House was still not over. Donna was in a foul mood and Beverly was not feeling much better.

'Those seagulls never stopped screeching all night,' she complained.

'If you can call it night!' Donna cut in.

'You could use ear-plugs,' Howard suggested with a smile. He was determined not to let being tired ruin his first day as Laird of the island. He was enjoying sitting at the head of an oak table so huge that it would have made their dining table back home look like a shelf.

'And a mask to keep out the light, I suppose?' Far from feeling at home Bev was feeling more uneasy every minute. The unfamiliar food was not helping.

But it was Donna who voiced her thoughts. 'I want hash-browns,' she declared when she saw the plate of food Flora had provided.

'I should be grateful for what you've got,' Howard suggested. 'I wouldn't think they'd know a hash-brown if one jumped up and bit them.'

Donna wrinkled her nose and prodded with her knife at a small, dark circle of meat which nestled amongst the bacon, scrambled eggs and fried bread. 'What is this?'

Howard was proud to air the knowledge he had taken so much trouble to read up before the trip. 'That's black pudding, of course.'

'*What* is black pudding.'

Howard relished the next bit. 'It's made from pig's blood.'

Donna cupped a hand over her mouth, went red in the face and fled from the table, only just making it to the cloakroom before she threw up.

Beverly, who was feeling very queasy too, said, 'I don't think that was very tactful, Howard.'

Howard was unrepentant. 'Bev, try some porridge, why don't you? It's great with salt instead of sugar. That's the proper way to eat it.'

Bev, growing irritated by her husband's determination to revel in his new surroundings, shook her head. 'No, thank you. If I ate that every day I'd end up larger than Flora.' She shivered and rubbed her palms along her blue, mohair-covered arms. 'It's cold around here.'

'That's why you need the porridge. Protects you against the cold winds of winter.'

'But, Howard, it's only summer. We will *have* to do something about the central heating system, if you can call it that!'

The system had been installed in the late 1930s by a rich Yorkshire mill-owner who had bought the island for his retirement, intending to spend the rest of his life fishing for trout. One winter of trying to cope with the boiler, which had grown even crankier in its old age, had driven him away for ever.

Howard glanced critically at the ornate but ineffective cast-iron radiators. 'I'll talk to MacPherson about it. There are a good many things that need seeing to. Looking through the accounts it seems to me this island is running well below its earning capacity. Things are run here the way they were in the dark ages.'

'I thought it was the history that attracted you to the place,' Beverly teased.

'History's all right and one thing it teaches you is to move with the times if you don't want to end up as a footnote.'

'If you'd like to check out some history, try the vacuum cleaner. Back home we've got items younger than that in museums.'

'Leave all that stuff to Flora. She's the housekeeper, that's what we're paying her for. You enjoy yourself.'

'Howard, I shan't enjoy myself until things are cleared up around here.'

Donna, white-faced, crept round the door.

'How's Momma's pet?'

'OK I guess.' She looked far from well. 'Mom, how long are we going to be here?'

Bev looked uncomfortable. The question had crossed her mind. 'That's up to your father. Why, honey?'

'Because I'm not sure I can live in a house with a willow-patterned john!'

Like most of the island children Shona had often been up to the Big House. Because it was usually uninhabited it was a great place to play but also, below the overgrown vegetable garden, apple trees thrived in the shelter of the orchard walls. Each September when the crop was ripe Shona and the others went up and collected pocketfuls of juicy fruit.

The Factor knew what went on but as long as no damage was done he did not mind. He would far rather they had the fruit than it should be left to fall off and rot when it would only provide food for flocks of blackbirds, thrushes and fieldfares.

That was how Shona was familiar with the gap where the stone wall had crumbled at the corner of the orchard furthest from the house.

The difference was that this time the apples were not ripe, the house was no longer empty and therefore she knew she had no right to be there.

She had walked along the beach, using the sand-dunes for cover, until she was level with the house but now she would have to come out and cross the open ground of the machair where she could easily be spotted.

She lay in the dune, her face pressed into the fine grains and gazed up at the Big House. It was so tall compared to most of the buildings on the island, which were single storeyed, and it had so many windows which gazed back at her. She watched each of them in turn for the slightest twitch of a curtain but saw none. Slowly, she hauled herself up to begin the long, exposed journey before she would gain the cover of the wall.

Trying to make herself smaller and less easy to see Shona tried to walk in a crouch, but for Shona walking upright was difficult enough and it made her progress over the uneven ground even slower.

With each step she took she expected to hear a voice call out, demanding to know where she was going, but nobody did and after what seemed like hours she arrived beside the gap. She sank down on a fallen stone in the shelter of the wall, breathless, frightened but thankful she had not been seen.

But she was, by the golden eagle. Having provided his young with an early breakfast of field mice and voles he was soaring high up in the perfect blue sky looking for more substantial prey. He had watched Shona's ragged progress towards the house and was not pleased.

The Big House, with its courtyard, buildings and over-grown garden, provided homes for hundreds of creatures usually undisturbed by humans and was a favourite hunting ground.

Not only was the girl at the foot of the orchard but a boy was making his way across the courtyard towards the rusty gate which led to the garden.

Lazily the eagle trimmed his great wings and glided off towards the solitude of the mountain slopes.

The rusty wrought iron gate squealed on its hinges as Carl forced it inwards against a bank of nettles. Once inside he had to use giant's strides to clear the thick network of purple brambles which criss-crossed the ground. His progress was slow and painful as their sharp thorns pierced his jeans and stabbed his flesh.

Shona froze when she heard the distant squeal of the gate. She was through the gap in the wall and was using the umbrellas of green leaves provided by the trees to hide her as she got closer to the house. Her cheek pressed against the smooth bark of an apple tree, she listened hard for more sounds. None came. Cautiously she crept on.

Carl was in trouble. The further he fought his way into the garden the tougher and thicker became the brambles. Now they not only scratched his legs, they caught and held threads of his thick yellow sweater. It was if hundreds of unseen fingernails were clawing at him trying to prevent him from reaching his objective, a smaller, but equally rusty gate that appeared to lead into an orchard.

34

Shona had her eye fixed on the same gate. She had never been through it but she knew where it led and expected, once inside it, to get a good view of the house. Slowly, tree by tree, she edged towards it. But she leapt back as somebody, or something, she could not tell which, crashed down with a sharp cry of pain just beyond the gate.

'Damn!' Carl cursed to himself. His sneaker had caught under a loop of bramble and he had fallen forwards into a thicket of brutal spikes. His face and hands were scratched and bleeding as the prickles obstinately clung to his clothes refusing to let him up. The more he tried to get out the more entangled he became but at last he was free.

Painfully pulling himself up he thought he caught a fleeting glimpse, through the bars of the gate, of a figure darting, uncertainly between the trees. Under the dappled shade it was hard to tell whether the figure was animal or human, so odd was the movement, and by the time he finally made it to the gate there was nothing to see or hear except the whisper of the breeze through the leaves and the distant hiss of surf.

What made everything worse was that the gate he had suffered so much to reach was held firm by a rusty chain and padlock. There was nothing for it but to fight his way back through the thicket of the garden.

Shona sat hunched in the shadow of the wall quivering with fright.

# Five

That night Shona was back on her usual perch above the quay when the 'school boat' tied up. It was the regular car-ferry but now it brought home, for their summer holidays, all the children who went to school on the mainland. Shona thought of it as the Pied Piper bringing back the children to Hamelin.

As the ship docked the children thronged the rails trying to catch first glimpses of their parents who were lined up on the quay trying to spot them too.

It seemed she had watched the 'school boat' coming home for as long as she could remember. But that night there was something different about it. In the past it had always been to do with other people but for the first time, whilst watching the ferry dock, Shona realised that when those children returned to the mainland school she might be standing at the rail waving goodbye to her parents. She had never in her life left the island and could not imagine doing so. Shona felt that that would be like giving up eating or breathing and a knot of fear tightened in her stomach.

Not only would she lose the freedom she enjoyed on the island but worse, she would lose the love and support of people, especially her mother and Dr MacGregor. She already knew how dreadful it was to lose Uncle James, but safe on the island she had all the others. On the mainland there would only be her brothers.

Shona had overheard whispered discussions about her going but the subject was changed the moment she entered the room. Not knowing whether she was going or not made it feel so much worse. Like an empty boat drifting.

Even from where she was Shona had no difficulty spotting her brothers. Their dark, wavy, red hair glowed like beaten copper in the evening sunlight. Shona was convinced she could count their freckles, they stood out so sharply.

She always viewed the return of Andrew and Sandy with mixed feelings. On the one hand the family felt more complete but, on the other, they always laid claim to so much of their mother's time. Shona knew that was unfair, they were only home for such a short while each time, but still she could not help resenting it.

Shona also realised she was an embarrassment to them. They would have denied it if asked but it was a fact. The other children brought schoolfriends from the mainland, particularly for the long summer holidays, but her brothers never had. Shona knew that was her fault, because they were ashamed of her.

They were never unkind to her. Unlike some of the other children, they never smirked at her behind their hands, or said hurtful things just within earshot. But she knew that whilst they would play with her at home, or somewhere private like the beach, they quietly preferred not to be seen around with her.

'Shona can't walk as fast as us,' Sandy used to explain to their mother, during the brief time they all three went to the island school, when the two boys always arrived home without her.

Shona knew that was not the real truth. Even if they left at exactly the same moment Sandy or Andrew would find an excuse to split off from her although, seconds later, they might be meandering along the road only metres ahead. But still that was far enough away not to be able to hear the taunts and catcalls that Shona's curious walk sometimes attracted from the crueller pupils.

In fairness she had to admit they would stop anybody saying anything unkind to her within their hearing and they had no mercy on anyone who bullied her.

Shona would never forget the day when Mary Taggart had deliberately pushed her over. Sandy had pounced on Mary like an angry tiger. He grabbed Mary's pigtail and pulled it until she screamed. Shona had thought Sandy was going to murder the girl. Miss Ferguson heard Mary's cries from inside the school and came out to rescue her but she had a hard job pulling Sandy away without scalping Mary in the process.

Sandy was made to spend the rest of the afternoon in disgrace with his face in a corner, but to Shona he had shone like a knight in armour. Yet later, when Shona had tried to thank him for standing up for her, he had shrugged it off, looking cross. It was as if he blamed Shona for what had happened and hated having to fight her battles for her.

Even so, the moment Sandy and Andrew set foot on the quay, after they had hugged their mother, their eyes searched the hill knowing Shona would be up there watching. The second they spotted her the boys waved like mad.

Shona managed to wave back, just too late for them to notice.

She watched her father bend his broad back to pick up the cases, which the boys had struggled with, as if each weighed no more than her mother's handbag. Then the four of them set off up the road, the boys shouting and laughing as they brought their parents up to date with the latest gossip and scandal from school. For a moment, as she watched them go she felt left out, forgotten, but she shrugged it off. She was happy to make her own way home.

Anyway, she might not go straight home. It was getting dark. What better time to go to the Big House than when they had their lights on but would not be able to see her?

As she toiled along she wished she knew the boy's name. So far she had not heard anybody use it and in any case they were more likely to call him 'the Laird's son' than anything else. But she would have felt that little bit closer to him knowing his name.

Halfway there she began to wonder if she had been wise

to set out. Not only was it totally dark but a cold wind was blowing up from the east.

Sometimes when it blew very hard from the east Shona would clamber to the top of the tallest hill she could manage and shout messages for Uncle James, hoping the wind might carry them to America. And, when the next westerly blew, she would struggle up the same hill to find out if he had got her message and sent one in return. Occasionally she truly believed that she could hear the murmur of his voice on the wind but she could no more make out his words than most people could understand hers.

Tonight she did not feel the urge to send a message. It was not the lack of strength in the wind but a feeling of harm in it which almost made her turn for home. But in spite of all these warning signs she kept on going.

What worried her even more was that the journey seemed to be taking longer than it should. She carried a very good sense of time and direction in her head. That was why her parents let her wander so freely. But she had been walking for over half an hour and there was no sign of the house.

Weird stories of houses being transported or, worse still, swallowed by a peatbog formed in her mind but she tried to dismiss them.

Much more frightening was the possibility that for once her sense of direction had failed her and she was lost. Perhaps *she* was in danger of being swallowed up by a bog!

Panic welled up inside her and lurched back and forth in her stomach like the crazy pendulum of a clock.

Being lost on the island, small as it was, was a very serious matter. It was peppered with traps for the unwary. Two years ago a tourist had lost his life in a quicksand. This year another tourist had spent several days in the cottage hospital recovering from the effects of exposure after being benighted on the moors despite having map and compass with him.

Shona knew that nobody would find her at this time of night, or know where to start looking.

She stood still. Tried to get her bearings from the

silhouettes of the land. Whilst it all seemed familiar there were no recognisable landmarks. She even began to doubt the direction of the wind. Maybe it was not a true easterly but one of those winds which swirl around, all the time coming from different points of the compass. If that was true she could have been walking in any direction. It was an eerie sensation. The roots of the hairs on the back of her neck stood out clear from her skin.

She could not persuade her feet to move. Always unruly, now they refused to obey her at all. Was she doomed to spend the rest of her life here? Pure fear sent an ice-cold trickle of sweat down between her shoulder blades.

Her eyes frantically raked the dim horizon for anything familiar, no matter how small.

And then she thought she saw the sign she was looking for!

Facing straight into the wind she caught sight of the faintest glimmer of golden-red, as if somebody over there was pouring red-hot metal.

Could it be the sunrise? If so it was a true east wind and she was not lost after all. Patiently she waited. The tiny glow grew and became more golden.

She heaved a sigh of relief as her panic began to subside and she set off confidently in the direction of the Big House, laughing at herself for being so easily tricked by the mystery of darkness. She knew exactly where she was now. There was a shallow, bowl-shaped valley just before the house. When she had panicked she was at the very bottom of the bowl and despite being only minutes away from her goal she could not possibly have seen it because it was hidden by the hill she was now climbing.

But when she got to the brow of the hill she realised her journey had been a complete waste of time. The house was in total darkness. Everybody had gone to bed. Shona felt so tired and deflated she wanted to cry but she kept on walking until she reached a clump of trees which separated the grass paddock from the beach, where she sat on a log to rest.

It was the only sizable plantation of trees on the island.

Elsewhere a few stunted hawthorn bushes were all that managed to survive and they all grew pointing sharply east, the way they had been forced by years of buffeting from the harsh, westerly, winter gales. During the winter their naked, spiky branches made Shona think of witches, their bodies buried beneath the ground, only their withered, gnarled arms and hands reaching out to clutch at anything that passed.

But here the Big House had given enough protection for oaks, birch, sycamores and holly to grow to a good height.

As Shona rested against the smooth, silver-grey bark of a sycamore she could not help wishing that it was her pillow and that she was safe at home in bed. She had just decided it was getting late and she ought to go when she thought she heard voices.

At first it did not surprise her. She had imagined so many things, what was one more?

But the voices were real and they were getting closer.

She slid round the trunk of the sycamore so that she was mostly out of sight but might see what was happening.

The voices were too low for her to hear what they were saying but as the figures slipped through the shadows of the trees she recognised the hunched shoulders of the Angus brothers. They were neither liked nor trusted by the islanders who suspected them of being behind all kinds of skulduggery.

As Shona's father often said, when something went wrong or missing, 'It's all in the hands of Fate or the Angus brothers!'

Not only were they devious but they were also frequently drunk, when they were apt to get into fights. Consequently most islanders, whilst they did not respect them, avoided them, especially late on Saturday nights. Then they would usually be seen staggering up the road, swigging from whisky bottles concealed in brown paper bags, which most self- respecting islanders left done up with string and only opened privately during the Sabbath when the pubs were not open.

Shona had good reason to know them. On many a Saturday night she had been woken by their singing and fighting in the lane outside. Often they would send their empty bottles crashing against the wall as they set off for home.

They lived just beyond Shona's home in a broken-down cottage on a thin finger of land that poked out into the sea. It had once been the boat-house belonging to the Big House. Then a fisherman and his wife had it, until it grew too dilapidated. It had got much worse since the Angus brothers moved in. The thatch was ragged and strewn with moss, the broken windows were stuffed with cardboard boxes and the door, which was left banging in all weathers, had sunk on its hinges.

They were known apart not by their names but by the colours of their hair, Red and Black. Nobody had ever talked to them long enough to discover their real names or where they came from. Incomers they were, who had arrived drunk on the ferry six years ago and had wandered round the island for a few days until they found the deserted cottage.

They had asked nobody's permission to move in and nobody had the courage to ask them to leave, not even the Factor. They paid no rent and did no work, for nobody would employ them but they got the money from somewhere to support their expensive drinking habits. After occasional visits to the mainland they drank more heavily. Nobody was sure if they had gone to the mainland to dispose of their ill-gotten gains or robbed somebody over there and returned to drink the proceeds. The Factor, like everyone else, suspected them of criminal activities but until he caught them at it there was nothing he could do.

Shona was certain their presence near the Big House could only mean they were up to no good. She pressed herself tight against the tree, terrified of what they might do to her if they caught her. They were so close she could hear the words they were muttering at each other.

'Och, it would be easy,' said one.

'We've kept out of trouble all this time . . .'

'But think of the money!'

'Aye, and think of the risk.'

'You're not afraid, are you?'

'You don't say that about me!'

They had stopped to argue right beside Shona's tree. She could smell the sour whisky on their breath. If she had stretched out her hand she could have touched their boots.

'Keep your voice down or you'll wake the district!'

'Nobody calls me a coward and gets away with it. Not even my own brother.'

'Calm down, will you? Just tell me why you won't do it?'

There was a brief pause. 'I'm not saying I won't. I'm just saying as it's risky, that's all.'

Shona heard no more. Having settled their differences their voices sank low and they began to move away. As she peered after them she was convinced that one had a rabbit slung over his shoulder, no doubt poached from somewhere close to the house.

She was left wondering what wickedness they were planning. Surely they could not intend to harm the Laird or his family? Bad as the brothers were nobody thought them capable of murder, except in the heat of a drunken brawl. No, murder was out of the question. What then? Robbery? The Laird was obviously a wealthy man.

Having made sure they were far enough ahead for there to be no danger of their turning and seeing her Shona set off for home, worrying about what she had heard and wondering what she could do about it.

The problem was she had heard so little and it was only because the conversation had taken place by the Big House that she had assumed the two were in some way connected. She could be completely wrong. But even supposing she was right there was no way she could get her story across, even to her mother.

She was so exhausted the last few metres to her home seemed to take an eternity. But her foot was barely on the path when the door swung open and her mother stood, hands on hips, looking very angry.

'And where've you been until this time? You've had us all worried sick. Your brothers have been in bed long since and your father's out scouring the island for you.'

Shona wanted to apologise, say she had not realised how late it was and that she had not meant to worry them. All she got out was, 'I--eeu-argoth.' Flustered she tried again. 'I--eeu-argoth.'

'You never mind all that,' her mother said impatiently, 'you'd best get to your bed before your father comes back, or he'll give you something to think about.' She propelled Shona firmly into the house. 'There's milk warming by the fire and some biscuits. I suspect you'd best take them to your bed or you'll not be finished by the time your father's home.'

Shona stroked her mother's arm. It was a gesture she often used and it expressed all kinds of things from 'I'm sorry' and 'thank you' to 'I love you'.

Her mother knew fine what it meant but worry had made her angry and she was in no mood to calm down yet. 'Sometimes I think you have no thought for others at all. You go wandering off for hours on end with us not knowing where you are and your brothers come home, wanting to see you.'

Shona stroked her arm again.

'Yes, well. You'd best be off to your bed.' She patted Shona's hair which was still damp from the night air. 'I'll bring a towel and dry your hair.

She was undressed and sitting up in bed when her mother brought through a plate of biscuits, a mug of milk and the towel. Gently she rubbed the hair dry and then, while Shona began to eat, she picked up the clothes which Shona had dropped where she stood.

'Aye, you're a trial at times and no mistake!' her mother said, but now the words were gentle and low.

Shona wondered if this was the moment to try to tell her about the Angus brothers and what she had heard but before she could order her thoughts and try to turn them into words her mother was kissing her good night and heading for the door.

'Off to sleep the moment you've finished mind.' And she was gone.

Shona lay awake long after her father had returned and gone to bed, worrying about what she had seen and heard but was powerless to do anything.

# Six

'You've painted the back door, at last,' Sandy called out.

'There's a new cover on my bed and orange curtains in our room,' Andrew chimed in.

It was like a treasure hunt, part of the ritual of coming home for the holidays, trying to find all the changes that had been made since they left.

Shona sat on her mother's knee to enjoy the search. Mr MacLeod always took breakfast with the boys on their first day home. He had said nothing about the wild goose chase Shona had had him on the previous night. Sometimes Shona wondered if he realised that she existed. She knew he worked very hard but whilst he seemed to make time for the boys he never did for her, not in the way that her mother or Uncle James had.

The only time he even gave her a cuddle was in the evening when he was smoking his pipe by the fire when Shona would slowly slide on to his lap with the stealth of a cat. Absentmindedly he would stroke her hair but the second he realised what he was doing he would find some excuse, such as checking the hen-house was closed, to get up.

Despite his gruff exterior Mr MacLeod was a soft-hearted man, willing to spend far more in vet's bills than any animal was worth to avoid its suffering. It pained him too deeply to watch Shona's heroic tussle with life but be powerless to help and so he turned his back on her. But the thought which haunted him constantly was what would happen to Shona if anything happened to him and his wife.

Beaming at the boys he said, 'Still two more to find.'

Sandy looked thoughtful. 'Morag is still here.'

'Aye,' his father confirmed. 'Though for how much longer we've yet to see.'

Andrew looked out through the window. 'You've not cut the hay already, have you?'

Mr MacLeod shook his head. 'I thought we'd save that for when you were back.'

Sandy and Andrew both looked baffled. Shona wriggled with pleasure for she knew what they had missed.

'Do you give up?' Mrs MacLeod asked. Reluctantly they both nodded. 'Well, I know fine you aren't keen on soap and water but I thought you might have noticed by now that we've a new sink put in here.'

The boys, disappointed by the revelation and downcast by their defeat in the game, both groaned.

'But you've still missed the most important change,' their father observed.

'What's that?' Sandy asked.

'The new Laird, of course!'

'Oh, that!' Sandy was scornful. 'I'm not going to bother my head about him.'

'There's not a person on this island, I'm thinking, that won't be bothered by him sooner or later.'

His wife shook her head at him. 'Don't fill their heads with all that on their first day home.'

But he continued as if he had not heard her. 'That man is a man for changes. I cannot see him letting things lie.'

Mother plumped Shona down so suddenly she almost fell. 'And you are a great one for seeing the black side. If we keep ourselves to ourselves he'll not be bothering with the likes of us.'

'Maybe,' he said, 'maybe.' But it was clear from his tone that he did not agree.


'Why don't you come out and explore today?' Carl asked his sister. He was still thrilled by his surroundings and anxious to show off his discoveries but his father was always busy with MacPherson and neither Beverly nor Donna had left the house since they arrived.

'My sinuses ache!' Donna replied.

Beverly glanced up from the copy of *Ms Magazine* she had had the foresight to bring with her and gave Donna a tolerant smile. 'Haven't you still got some of your tablets Dr Leibman prescribed?'

Donna thrust her chin out. 'They don't seem to work here. Nothing seems to work here.'

'Maybe there's a local remedy.'

Donna wrinkled her nose with disgust. 'Mixed by three witches on a blasted heath, I suppose?'

That was too much, even for Beverly. 'They *do* have doctors here, you know!'

To Carl it was clear that Donna's sinus problems were largely imaginary, mainly an excuse not to have to leave the house. Her behaviour reminded him of their cat, Ronnie, the time they had moved from Chicago to New York. Though the cat was curious about its new surroundings it could not summon up the courage to go out. For hours on end it crept round the walls, first of one room then another, crouched low, fur bristling, uttering a loud, low-pitched whine. It refused to walk across the open space of the carpet. This went on for days until Ronnie had checked out the exact dimensions and methods of escape from every room. Only when it was totally familiar with its new home would it set paw outside and then the cat went through a similar routine in the garden.

But once Ronnie had felt comfortable he ruled the district like Attila the Hun.

'Maybe I'll try to fix up my room,' she said but the tone of voice suggested it was well beyond mere fixing! She put her chin on her hand and let out a melodramatic sigh. 'I bet Bruno and Pattie are having a great time back home.'

Carl attempted to cheer her up. 'I found some sort of cart in one of the outhouses.'

Donna's eyebrows shot up and disappeared under a carefully arranged, tousled, fringe. 'A cart? What on earth would I do with a cart?'

Carl shrugged. 'I just thought if there was a cart around there must be horses on the island. When we went to New York you complained how much you missed riding. Maybe Dad could get you a horse and you could ride here.' He saw the look of panic in her eyes.

'How could I go riding with my sinuses hurting like this?'

Carl, seeing that nothing was going to please, gave up. 'Well, I'm off out.'

Beverly looked up. 'What are you going to do?'

He held up his dad's binoculars and a bird book he'd unearthed in the musty library. 'I'm going twitching.'

'Twitching?' His mother looked amused. Always fascinated by quaint, local customs, she asked, 'What's that?'

'Bird-watching, well, bird spotting to be exact. Did you know the guide book says there are over eighty species of bird on this island?'

'Who cares!' Donna said with heavy scorn.

'I do,' Carl replied with a cheerful grin. 'I've made a list and I'm going to see how many I can spot while I'm here. Why don't you come too, Donna? See who spots most.'

'That certainly would be something to tell the folks back home!' Donna was pouring on the sarcasm. ' "What did you *do* out there all the time?" – "Oh, it was really wild. I saw over eighty sorts of birds!" That would really make them over-excited!'

'Donna!' Beverley slapped her magazine down. 'Don't be so childish.'

Donna gave up in disgust. 'Well, I ask you!'

'Do you want to come, Mom?'

'I'd love to but I've got things to see to around the place. There's such a lot needs fixing.'

Carl nodded knowingly. 'Sure, Mom, see you later.'

The second Carl was out of the room Donna went on the attack. 'Why did you let Daddy drag us off into this backwoods?'

'Donna! I don't *control* your father.'

This was true. She normally never argued with Howard but agreed with him over everything, particularly when their views coincided. Otherwise she worked on the 'give-him-enough-rope' principle believing that his wilder enthusiasms would quickly fade. In this case the fading was not yet apparent but she was still hopeful.

Donna persisted. 'But what made him do it? Is it some kind of mid-life crisis?'

Beverly could not resist a smile. 'You know he's always been passionate about his Scottish ancestry. Don't you remember all the effort and money he put into getting the family tree filled out?'

'Sure seems weird with a name like Kleinberger!'

'Yes,' agreed Beverly, 'but his mother's name was Stewart.'

'But she didn't come from this dump,' Donna protested, 'they came from some place near Glasgow that was so awful they pulled it down.'

'The Gorbals. Yes, I'm afraid that like a good many Americans his family didn't leave home because they wanted to. Poverty drove them out.'

'When he first told us we were coming to Scotland I kind of thought it would be some kind of . . .' her voice trailed off.

'Castle?' Beverly helpfully suggested.

'Yes.'

'And would that have made it better?'

'At least we could have suffered in style. This place is just . . . old. What made him choose it?'

'He happened to see an advertisement in a magazine which simply said, "Own Your Own Scottish Island!". He read it and he was hooked. It also happened at a time when he was having a little difficulty with the UK Inland Revenue. You know Daddy has money tied up in UK businesses?'

Donna nodded, though in truth she knew nothing of how her father made his money except that there had always been enough of it to keep her in a style which, until now, she had enjoyed.

'I don't understand the detail but Howard said there was a pile of money stuck over here which he'd be foolish to take back to the States because he'd be taxed twice. Anyway, when he came up with the idea of buying this island Glen, his whizz-kid accountant, jumped at it. So, here we are.'

Donna made a mental note to kill Glen if she ever met him. 'You don't mean we're stuck here for the rest of our lives, do you?'

'Don't be silly, Donna,' Beverly drawled in a voice which lacked its usual conviction. 'Of course not.'

Andrew and Sandy were kicking a ball about on the beach. They were trying to include Shona who could only kick a ball when it was still, which was not really football, but it was the first day of the holidays and they were feeling generous. Besides which there wasn't anyone else for them to play with. All the other children of their age had only just arrived home too. There was no novelty, yet, in going round to see people with whom they spent the whole school year.

Soon enough they would be occupied around the croft. Their father had not been joking about saving the hay harvest for them! Then there would be peat to cut, fences to mend, sheep to shear apart from work on the fishing boat.

So they were glad enough to take advantage of a free day and eager to get out of the house while their mother tutted her way through the contents of their suitcases.

'Come on, Shona, kick it!' Sandy urged.

Shona's mind was elsewhere. Way up the beach in the sand-dunes she had spotted the blond head of a boy.

'What are you staring at?' Andrew demanded.

Shona did not want to tell him. It was her secret and she preferred to keep it to herself. She knew that secrets tend to change once they get shared, especially with brothers.

Reluctantly she raised her arm and pointed in the direction of the blond-haired boy who seemed to be hiding.

Andrew shaded his eyes with his hand. 'Looks like a boy.'

'Who is it?' Sandy asked.

Shona tried to form the words, 'Laird's son', but somehow they got mangled. 'Slair,' was all she could say.

Andrew ignored her. 'It's nobody we know.'

A mischievous grin spread across Sandy's face. 'Maybe it's one of the tourists' kids.'

Shona shook her head but the brothers were too wrapped up in their own thoughts to notice.

'Do you think we could have some fun with him?' Sandy wondered.

Shona began to hop up and down. They could not know that this was the Laird's son they were going to 'have fun with' and it could only lead to trouble. She tried to warn them but from her throat came only strangled sounds which they misunderstood.

'We'll play with you in a minute, Shona, be still!' Sandy said without even bothering to look at her but waving her away as if she were a horse-fly.

'Remember what Dad said about not bothering visitors,' Sandy warned.

'We aren't going to do him any harm, are we?' Andrew looked innocent.

Sandy was uncomfortable. 'No,' he said uncertainly.

'Just a bit of fun, that's all. Where's the harm, in that? Shona, stop pulling my arm. Can't you see we're busy?'

In a desperate attempt to get their attention Shona had forced her way between the boys and was tugging at Andrew's jumper.

He snatched the jumper away, ignoring the agonised expression on her face, as he began to make for the dunes. 'Come on, Sandy!'

'Eo-o-owgh!' Shona wailed after them.

Sandy paused long enough to shout over his shoulder, 'Back in a wee bit, Shona.' Then he disappeared behind the sand-dunes running after his brother.

For a moment Shona stood, abandoned on the beach. But then it crossed her mind that here was the very chance she had been looking for to get close to the boy. She could not resist it. Knowing that the scramble up the dunes would waste time she set off to limp down the beach, her eyes fixed on the head of the distant, unsuspecting boy.

Carl had had a good day. He did not know much about birds but with the help of the pictures in the book he had managed to identify two species of seagull, terns, shelduck and some eider ducks. When he was more experienced he would get to know the smaller birds like turnstones and dunlin which he barely noticed running along amongst the pebbles by the edge of the water. Similarly he would extend his vision. Instead of always looking in one direction he would learn to look around him. That way he would have noticed the broad wings of the golden eagle which soared above him. Certainly the eagle had noticed him.

The eider duck, which were floating about in the edge of the sea, gave him trouble. He could not stop himself thinking of them as eiderdowns, which set him off giggling so that he kept misting up the lenses of the binoculars. It got worse when he noticed in the book that there also King Eiders. Presumably for king-sized beds!

All the same he was having a good time spotting the birds and crossing them off on his list. Only seventy-five more to go!

'Donna should have come. The eiderdowns are neat!' he said to himself, and began giggling all over again.

Shona's wail interrupted him. He thought it must be a strange bird cry. Anxious not to miss a new species for his check-list he swung the binoculars in the direction of the sound.

'Oh, no!' he said out loud as he saw a strange girl waving her arms about as she walked almost crab-wise along the beach towards him. 'She'll scare off all the birds!'

As he spoke a flock of terns angrily threw themselves into the air and began screaming and wheeling round her head in an attempt to drive her away from their nests. Alerted by the terns the eider ducks beat the water with their wings as they taxied off. Only the larger shelduck seemed unconcerned.

Carl shouted at the girl. 'Go away, you stupid kid!'

'What did you say?' Andrew demanded.

Carl, startled out of his wits, rolled over on one elbow and was astonished to see two red-headed boys standing over him. 'She's frightening all the birds away,' he protested.

'Is that a fact?' Andrew spoke quietly but looked very angry. 'And what did you call my sister?'

Carl shrugged. 'Nothing. It was just an expression.'

'I heard you. You said, "stupid kid".'

Carl, hearing the ominous tone of the boy's voice, felt at a disadvantage lying in the sand. He struggled to his feet. When he was standing the angry one, although about Carl's age, was a little taller than him and looked a good deal tougher.

Shona was still some metres away but she could see her brothers talking to the Laird's son. Although she could not hear what Andrew was saying, it was clear, from the stiff way he held himself that he was angry.

She was convinced he was about to do something stupid which they would all regret. If only she was close enough to hear what was being said! If only she had been able to warn him about who the boy was!

In her attempt to hurry she lost her footing in the loose sand and almost fell on her face.

Anger and frustration brought on partly by her uncontrollable body but mainly by her brother flushed through her. She sensed he was about to start a quarrel with the Laird's son which would not only lead to trouble with the Laird, as well as their own father, but which would ruin the meeting with the boy which Shona had been dreaming about. And all because she could not get to them quickly enough to prevent the argument.

The next thing she saw was Andrew grabbing hold of the boy's sweater. The boy tried to push him away with a playful swing of his arm. Andrew, mistaking it for a punch, dodged the boy's arm and drove his own clenched fist into the boy's stomach. The boy folded up like the blade of a penknife being snapped shut and rolled around in agony in the sand.

Shona, certain that Andrew was about to pounce on him, shouted wordless sounds into the air and waved her arms wildly.

To her amazement Andrew stopped and dropped his hands to his sides but he was not looking at Shona, he was looking towards Sandy.

Sandy had noticed the Factor's familiar white Range Rover bumping along the sandy track which ran parallel with the dunes. The car pulled up and out jumped not only MacPherson but a stocky man in a blue baseball hat and tartan trousers. Sandy had seen enough American films to know that this could easily be the father of the boy rolling in agony on the sand whom Andrew was about to jump on.

'Andy!' he shouted. 'Look who's coming!'

Andrew looked up, saw and heard Shona shouting at him from the beach and then realised Sandy was looking the opposite way. Following his gaze he also saw the man with MacPherson charging across the machair towards them.

'Hey, you, MacLeod! Stop that!' MacPherson roared.

Shona arrived at the sand-dune from the beach at the moment the Factor and the Laird got to Andrew. The blond boy was struggling to his feet still clutching his aching stomach.

The Laird walked straight up to his son. 'Carl, are you OK?'

'Carl,' thought Shona. 'At least I know his name, although after this we're hardly likely to meet again.'

Carl looked in a sorry mess. His rumpled hair was full of sand, his glasses hung half off but he did not seemed pleased by his father's concern.

'I'm fine, Dad,' he managed to grunt. He was starting to get his breath back from Andrew's devastating blow.

MacPherson who had stood watching, his cheeks sucked in, decided it was time to play his part. 'MacLeod, I shall be having a word with your father about this.'

Andrew and Sandy stirred the sand with their toes and said in chorus, 'Yes, Mr MacPherson.'

Carl tried to interrupt. 'Will that be necessary?' But only Shona was listening.

Andrew was trying to make things better. 'It was only a bit of fun.'

MacPherson went puce and exploded. 'Fun? Behaving like a hoodlum? Attacking the Laird's son.'

Andrew's mouth dropped open. 'The Laird?' he gasped.

The Laird looked decidedly uncomfortable. He was used to dealing with trouble amongst the staff. But these kids were not staff. It was one kid thumping another. Happened all the time back home, particularly to Carl! He had warned him about keeping his guard up hundreds of times but the kid never learned.

Though he did not quite know how to stop him, Howard could not help feeling that MacPherson was over-reacting. Howard found it hard to accept being treated like visiting royalty. Especially when being watched so closely by the strange, silent, young girl who had not spoken but who made him feel even more uneasy.

Howard cleared his throat loudly. 'I guess you'd better pick up your things, Carl, and let's get going. Time's money.'

As she watched Carl picking up his book and shaking the sand from the pages she could not help wondering about that expression. She knew time could be long or short. In school sometimes it dragged but when things you enjoyed ended suddenly it seemed too short. Perhaps 'time's elastic' would be better. From Shona's experience of her parents' life they never had enough time and for them only *work* was money.

Reminded of time Mr MacPherson glanced at his watch. 'Weren't you meeting those men about your computers about now?' The stress he put on the word 'computer' suggested not a piece of technical equipment but an open sewer.

But Carl's face brightened visibly. 'See you guys!' he

56

growled with as much dignity as he could muster and followed his father back to the car.

MacPherson hung back looking directly at Sandy and Andrew. 'Tell your father I'll be up to see him this evening on my way home,' he said, and without waiting for a reply he turned on his tan brogues to follow the laird.

'That's torn it!' Andrew said, the second MacPherson was out of earshot. 'Fine holiday this is going to be!'

# Seven

Nothing was said during the journey back to the Big House. Neither Carl nor his father wanted to talk about it in front of Mr MacPherson.

'Will you be needing me after lunch, Mr Kleinberger?' he asked as he brought the Range Rover to a halt by the front door. Flora's husband Donald Henderson had spent the morning unjamming the lock.

'No, I don't think so, maybe tomorrow and we can go over some of those figures for the deer.'

'Certainly, sir. Would you like Henderson here too?'

'Henderson?' Howard, who prided himself on knowing not only the name of everybody who worked for him but their precise function, had to admit he was still struggling with the names of the islanders. It was particularly difficult because so many were inter-related and shared the same family name. 'Why do we need the handyman with us?'

'Not Donald Henderson. Dougal. He manages the herd.'

Howard tried to cover his embarrassment. 'No, that won't be necessary tomorrow.'

'As you wish,' MacPherson leant forward to start the car.

'There is just one other thing,' Howard said, sounding uncomfortable. 'Would you leave the car here this afternoon? I might take Mrs Kleinberger for a drive round the island.'

MacPherson, who had so far been chauffeuring Howard around and was therefore able, to some extent, to control what his boss saw, was not entirely happy with that idea. 'I'd be happy to drive you,' he offered.

'That's very kind of you but I *can* drive and you have more important things to do, I'm sure.'

'As you wish.' He was also sad to lose the use of the more comfortable Range Rover which he had enjoyed almost exclusively for years. He was not looking forward to using his tired old mini again. 'Tomorrow at ten then? And I'll have a word with MacLeod on my way home.'

'You know best, MacPherson, but take it easy on the kid, will you?'

As they walked into the hall Howard put his hand on Carl's shoulder. 'You want to keep out of trouble with the locals, kid.' Carl was about to protest that the whole thing had arisen out of a misunderstanding which was mainly his fault but his father continued, 'Scraps like that could make life very uncomfortable for me. Understand me? And next time the cavalry might not arrive in time.'

His father's suggestion that he was unable to take care of himself hurt Carl almost as much as Andrew's punch. He nodded.

'Now I've got to see these guys about getting a computer terminal set up here.'

Carl's eyes lit up. 'A terminal?'

'Sure. I enjoy isolation but not up to the point where it could ruin me. I need electronic mail, fax, the whole shooting match so that I can stay in touch with London and New York. Glen has been organising a package and these guys are here to talk over the details.'

Carl was about to ask if he could sit in on the discussions when the sitting room door opened and Beverly came out. 'There you are, Howard. I've been enjoying a fascinating discussion about computers but I think these nice gentlemen would prefer to talk to you.'

Howard went into the sitting room and shut the door before Carl had chance to speak.

Beverly smiled at Carl. 'Having a good time, honey?'

'Sure, Mom,' he said and went up to his room.

*

For once, mainly because the boys were so reluctant to get home at all, Shona arrived home with them.

Their mother was at the back of the house scattering handfuls of corn for the hens.

'My, you're back early. I wasn't expecting to see you until your stomachs brought you home.' She threw the last handful of grain and, whilst the hens pecked away at it, went over to the back of the hen-house to take the eggs from the nesting-boxes. 'I've baked a fruit cake. You can have some when I finish this.'

'I'm not very hungry,' said Andrew.

'Don't give me shocks like that, young man! You'll have me dropping these eggs. You not hungry – are you sickening for something?'

Andrew's serious face and the silence of the other two quietened her. 'Where's Dad?' he asked.

'Making a start on the hay. Why?'

'I've got into some trouble. Mr MacPherson is coming to talk to Dad about it tonight.'

Shona sat by her bedroom window with her chin on her hand gazing out at the beautiful day which was ending so badly after such a promising start.

When Mr MacLeod had laid aside his scythe and come back to the house for lunch Andrew had explained the reason for Mr MacPherson's intended visit. He told his father that he had got into a fight with the Laird's son without mentioning, in front of Shona, the cause of it. Sandy did not explain. His father was going to be angry enough anyway, he wanted as little share in it as possible.

Mr MacLeod had confined all three of them to the house for the rest of the day. As their mother had decided the whole house would need a clean through for the Factor's visit they were stuck in their bedrooms. Which was not so bad for the boys, Shona thought, they at least had each other for company.

Shona was getting bored. It was late afternoon. She knew her father had milked Morag. She had seen him coming back towards the house with the pail of milk. She could hear him banging about in their bedroom, no doubt reluctantly changing into his Sunday suit ready for the Factor's visit.

She had spent the afternoon going through her treasure box. It was an old cigar box which she had found on the beach. Inside were a photograph of Uncle James taken the day he left the island, and some of the favourite stones and shells she had collected from the beach but one thing was missing. Her piece of flawed glass.

It was the end broken off a bottle, its jagged edges worn smooth by the action of the sea, which she had picked up off the beach when she was young. It was a rather unusual shade of bluey-green and Shona loved looking through it. Not only when she was happy but at times like this, when everything had gone wrong, because looking through the lumpy, bubbly glass changed her view of the world entirely.

In many ways she felt that she had much in common with that old piece of glass. Just as the images that entered the glass were changed, not always for the better, by the time they got through it, so it was with her. Capable of receiving the most complex information she could not make use of it to the point at which she could tell anyone what she knew or felt.

Otherwise she could have warned Andrew about Carl so that they would not have ended up in father's bad books.

But where was the piece of glass?

She tipped everything out of the box. The flower she had picked and pressed after her first day at school, half a blue-grey swan's egg she had found and kept for the powdery smoothness of it were still there but her piece of glass was missing. Nothing was valuable but everything was irreplaceable.

As she gazed through the window she wished she had been able to find the glass. She enjoyed looking at the sky through it, particularly if there was a fiery sunset.

A movement beyond the cow byre caught her eye. It was somebody coming down the track. Surely not Mr

MacPherson on foot? No, that was impossible. In any case he was coming in the wrong direction.

Shona pressed her face flat against the cold glass of the window and saw Red Angus disappearing behind the end of the house.

She shot awkwardly out of her bedroom, bumping into her mother in her hurry to get to the front window.

'You nearly had me over! What in Heaven's name is the matter with you, Shona?'

But Shona was too busy watching to see if Red Angus was going towards the Big House or not. In all the excitement and upset of Andrew's fight she had almost forgotten the conversation she had overheard the previous night.

Thankfully he did not stick to the track but turned off at right angles to it, heading for the mountain. No doubt off to do some more poaching.

'What is it, Shona?'

Before Shona could reply she realised there *was* somebody coming down the track. It looked like a miniature whirlwind heading for the croft. The dust storm was being created by an old mini.

Mrs MacLeod came to see what Shona was pointing at. 'My, it's the Factor,' she said with an ill-concealed smile. 'And just look at that contraption he's driving. We have come down in the world! He'll not be pleased about that!'

The female golden eagle accepted her lot, minding the chicks while the male went hunting. Though she looked forward to the days when the eaglets would be old enough to be left alone without being in danger from marauding hooded crows and hungry magpies, willing to feed off any bird's chicks or eggs. All day she was beset by them, diving and wheeling above the nest. The sight of her chicks, plump in their nest was too much for them. They had tried time and time again to distract her so that they might swoop in from behind, scoop up a tasty chick and still escape her vicious beak and talons. But whilst they had cheek enough for an army, they lacked the courage to carry out their plan.

Reluctantly they had given up the struggle, wandered off for easier pickings, and left her in peace with her chicks.

But something new had come to disturb her. A red-headed man skirted the base of the mountain and then started the ascent of the lower slopes. She had often seen him before when he came to set snares for rabbits. Sometimes they had plucked an already dead rabbit from its infernal grasp before the man came up to collect it.

But they had no love for each other this man and the golden eagle.

Sometimes when he came to check the snares he stood and watched the eagles in flight. They tried to mislead him about the site of their nest, flying away in an attempt to draw him off from the Black Mountain, but during the hatching of the eggs he climbed all the way to the top, even though the male had dived at him to drive him back. The man had hidden behind a boulder metres from the nest, peering at the female as she sat her eggs, fluffing herself out and crouching down in a fruitless attempt to blend in more with her surroundings.

Although he had gone away and not bothered them again until now, his presence gave her an uneasy feeling. With her beak she stirred the noisy chicks into a safe group behind her, silenced them with a low sound they knew meant danger, and waited as the red-haired man began the climb. He was already well beyond his last snare.

She searched the sky for the male eagle who had gone hunting. If he saw what was happening and returned they might stand something of a chance. If not . . . there was no knowing what the red-headed man intended.

'Mr MacLeod, I think you would do well to remember that we are dealing with a new Laird.' Mr MacPherson was standing next to the mantelshelf as if he owned it, which was not far from the truth.

The three children were ranged along the sofa under the window, still and silent as china ornaments.

Their parents sat stiffly at either end of the kitchen table which was unusually clear apart from the best china tea things which lay untouched. The fruit cake the children had been promised before all this occurred lay uncut. Mr MacPherson on his arrival had even refused the offer of tea, thinking the occasion too serious.

'I'm aware of that, Mr MacPherson.'

'Then I think you would do well to impress it upon your children. This morning's display of unwarranted violence did you no good whatsoever in his eyes.'

'I am aware of that too, Mr MacPherson.'

Mr MacPherson, long, thin hand stretched out before him, examined the ends of his fingernails. 'It is possible that the new Laird may see fit to make certain alterations.'

'Alterations, is it?'

'It is his right.'

'I don't deny that, Mr MacPherson. It's to be expected.'

'He has certain plans for, how shall I put it . . . ?'

'As plainly as possible, if you please, Mr MacPherson.'

'Certain changes of emphasis. For making aspects of the island more viable. More profitable.'

'Thank you, Mr MacPherson. I know fine what viable means.'

Mr MacPherson cleared his throat. 'The additional sheep grazing rights you enjoy . . .'

Mr MacLeod's eyes narrowed. 'Ah, yes. I wondered about those.'

'I think they are due for renewal,' he paused to emphasise the point, 'or not, on Lammas Day. Which is about a month away.'

'That's right. Last time we spoke you saw no problem.' MacPherson nodded. 'But now some question mark arises in your mind?'

MacPherson looked astonished. 'Not in my mind! It has nothing to do with me, you understand. If it were left to me there would be no problem.'

'I catch your drift. This morning's business with the young fellow has blackened the MacLeod name in the Laird's eyes and for that he would consider not allowing me the extra grazing I've had these last thirty years, and my father and grandfather before me, without which this croft would no longer be *viable*.'

Mr MacPherson smiled and having firmly planted the idea in Mr MacLeod's mind he knew he must now deny all knowledge of it. After all he had only dreamt up the idea as a way of putting pressure on the MacLeods to behave. He had gone much further than the Laird had in mind. 'I am saying nothing of the kind, Mr MacLeod. I was merely trying to indicate to you the need for caution. What the Laird calls "a low profile", at a time when change is in the air.'

'I'd be interested to know what new use the Laird would have for the side of a mountain and some lochans.'

MacPherson thought quickly and lit upon the subject he was to discuss with the Laird the following day. 'An extension of the deer herd.'

'I see. Of course the most he could expect is one more deer for every three of my sheep he takes off.'

'It is not just a question of *more* deer. It's the fence.'

Mr MacLeod looked concerned. 'There is no fence.'

'Not yet, no,' agreed Mr MacPherson.

'He would need a fine, long fence that would cut the island almost in half. It seems to me the deer have done well enough roaming the island as they have. Especially in the bad winters, when they come and eat on my land too.'

'But if they were contained it would improve the shooting.'

'And to contain them he would have to turn my sheep off and build something like the Berlin Wall across the island.'

'He can make more money from the deer than he can from the rents you are paying for that land. Even more when the shooting is improved.'

Mr MacLeod's face was grim. 'I, on the other hand, would be destitute, this being one of the smallest crofts on the island.'

'Your ancestors depended more on the fishing.'

'Which is more for the pot than the market these days, the

more so since my brother James is gone. If I don't have that land for my sheep I must quit. Is that what you want?'

'Mr MacLeod! It has not come to that yet. I am merely warning you that whilst change is in the wind these are not times to draw attention to your family in the way that your son did today. That is all. The Laird is looking at a number of proposals which in the end could benefit everyone on the island.'

'And turn me into a ghillie, earning a living from helping rich men to shoot deer on a few days a year!'

Mr MacPherson shrugged helplessly. 'I sincerely hope it will not come to that, Mr MacLeod.'

'Not as fervently as I do, Mr MacPherson.'

MacPherson glanced at his watch. 'I must go. I bid you good evening. Mrs MacLeod, thank you for the offer of tea, perhaps some other time.'

Mrs MacLeod smiled sweetly. 'Sometime around Lammas Day perhaps?'

'Er – yes, perhaps. My, the young girl is growing fast these days, isn't she?'

Shona dug her fingernails into the sofa. The people she hated most were those who talked in front of her as if she were deaf, dumb and stupid. Never addressing a single remark to her but always to some third party.

'She'll be joining her brothers on the mainland after the holidays, I suppose?' he asked Mrs MacLeod without a glance at Shona.

'It seems we all might, the way the wind is blowing just now, Mr MacPherson.'

'We must hope it does not come to that. Good-night.' He turned abruptly and left before anyone could see him to the door.

Once Mr MacPherson was outside and confronted by the sight of his bedraggled mini he had a moment to reflect on the changes that were affecting them all before he drove it off.

The children did not move. Only Mrs MacLeod got up to clear away the best china and pour mugs of tea for herself and her husband.

Andrew was the first to find his voice. 'I'm sorry, Dad, I didn't mean to bring all this trouble on you.'

Mr MacLeod waved the boy's apology away. 'It isn't anything to do with what you have done. Though that was daft enough in itself. No, it goes beyond that. We've all known changes were coming, it's just that I'm none too happy to find myself trawled up in their net.'

As the hand came over the edge of the nest the eagle pecked at it with the hooked tip of her beak.

Although the hand was gloved in thick leather her neck had tremendous strength. The leather was deeply scored by the beak and the hand inside the glove severely bruised.

The man cried out in hurt anger.

Her chicks, sensing the danger and aware of the tension in their mother's strong body, squealed to each other while she uttered shrill yelps of alarm.

For a moment the man's feet scrabbled on the mountainside directly under the nest sending a flurry of loose stones clattering down to the bottom. Then he got a toehold and once more eased himself up towards the nest, higher this time. His face appeared over the edge.

He had covered his red hair with a blue, knitted hat but nothing covered his pink-rimmed, watery blue eyes. They were the target for a swift, sharp movement of her beak. Though she missed his eyes she scored his cheek. He cried out with pain as the flesh split and blood spurted between his fingers. Clutching his injured face, he staggered back and lost his footing.

He pitched and rolled for twenty metres down the steep slope and was only brought to a bone-crunching halt by a sharp, pointed rock. He lay still for a moment, groaning and feeling parts of his body, as he tried to calculate the damage. Nothing was broken. His hand and face were still the most damaged parts though he also had severe bruising on his back and elbow, which was badly grazed where the rock had ripped his sleeve. But worse, his dignity was badly damaged too and he had grown very angry, a deadly combination.

The eagle gripped the edge of her nest with her talons. The chicks, still safe, sheltered behind her. High above her she heard the bleak alarm note of her mate: 'twee-oh' followed by sharp, brief barking cries.

She still did not feel confident of victory. Behind her the chicks were panicking, scuttering back and forth around the nest, squealing as they tumbled over each other.

The man had got up but was not going away. Slowly, hand over hand, he hauled himself back up the slope. On the way up he found a thin branch from a dead hawthorn and grasped it to use as a weapon.

Whilst the female continued to issue her thin yelps the male saw the man getting closer to the nest and with a loud 'twee-oh' swooped at him. At the last second the male pulled back, just as he would over a fleeing rabbit, and extended his talons. He was screaming down towards the back of the man, his head poised, talons thrust forward, ready to claw the flesh from the intruder's bones.

The man, angry and fearful but still determined, was wildly beating the stick above his head as he crawled into the shelter of the high ledge on which the nest was built.

The swooping eagle could not alter the angle of his dive to one acute enough to get in under the ledge without dashing himself to pieces against the rocks. He turned off sharply in a swift flurry of feathers. The turn was so late that the primary feathers of his right wing, which stood out like great fingers, brushed the man's back.

But the man still had not given up. While he inched out from under the ledge, reaching closer and closer to the nest, the male swooped back and forth as fast as his size and the restricted space would allow to try to drive him off.

The man, almost at the nest despite anything the two agitated birds could manage, had paused to remove his jacket which he swirled round and round his hand and then suddenly thrust straight at the female.

Furiously she attacked the swathed hand with beak and talons. Ripping, tearing, shredding the material with all her might, without realising that this was exactly what the man had intended. While she was occupied his other hand snatched up one of the chicks and in seconds the man had dived back down under the protection of the ledge.

The distraught birds cried and flapped their wings but they knew that nothing they could do would ever get their chick back into the nest.

Having recovered his breath the man, bleeding profusely from several places, had put on the tattered remains of his coat with the scrabbling, frightened chick imprisoned in a press-studded pocket, and was taking himself down the mountain as fast as he could, still whirling the branch above his head to dissuade any further attacks.

The male eagle still made angry passes above the man's head, banking and turning steeply, but knew it was pointless.

The female, outraged, angrily picked at the outer sticks of the nest whilst the two remaining chicks fought over their extra space. She could not help noticing that the weakest chick was still in the nest; the man had made off with the strongest of her brood.

Back in the bracken and almost on level ground Red Angus was calculating, in bottles of whisky, how much his mainland contact would pay for a golden eagle chick, destined to be reared on choicest meats and become the prized possession of a rich Arab prince whose passion was falconry.

# Eight

'I think we should all go for a drive round the island,' Howard announced as Dr MacGregor drove off.

'But there's such a lot to do round the house,' protested Beverly.

'Nothing that won't keep. Isn't that what the doctor said, Donna? Get outside into the good fresh air?'

Donna twisted her lip. 'What does he know? He probably isn't even a proper doctor.'

'Oh, I don't think that's at all fair, Donna,' Beverly protested. 'He spent time at Fort Worth and he has a brother who lives in Houston.'

Howard was firm. 'Come on everybody, we've done little else but work since we got here. I think it's time to lighten up.'

Even Carl had other ideas. 'Can't I stay and help the guys installing the computer system?'

'They won't be starting the interesting bit for days. Thanks to your mother!'

'I just didn't want all that junk in the house, is all.'

Donna gave a wicked grin. 'Nothing from the twentieth century would fit in with this Adams Family decor anyway!'

'That certainly wasn't what I meant, Howard!' Beverly protested. 'It's normally difficult enough to get you to stop work, it could only be worse having those machines in the house.'

'But they'll only be across the courtyard in the coach house,' Carl pointed out, 'that's hardly a day's journey.'

'Just far enough,' said Beverly.

'I only hope those builders MacPherson's hiring can get the place in shape quickly enough. You have to be so damned careful criticising anyone around here in case it's their third cousin, twice removed on their mother's side you're insulting, but I need the whole network up and running by the end of the week.'

'I will be able to use the word processor and the computer, won't I?' Carl wanted to be certain of his ground. With Donna it was always 'yes' to get her off his back but for Carl there always seemed to be grey areas.

'Sure!' Howard said. 'Now, let's all get in the car and go for a trip round the island!'

He was clearly not in a mood to argue. Beverly got up. 'We'd better all put warm clothes on.'

'I hope you realise I'll suffer for this tomorrow,' Donna moaned as she left the room.

Howard and Carl grinned privately at each other.

The female eagle, who still suffered feelings of outrage and violation, fussed round the edge of the nest making unnecessary adjustments to the sticks and leaves.

The chicks were fighting over the last scraps of meat. The strongest chick got most and the female eagle could see, now that it had become a straight two-way scrap, the smaller chick would get the worst of the deal. When there had been three, the weaker chick had often snatched up the very morsel over which the other two were fighting.

The male eagle soared above the nest. He had no sense of failure. Had it been a lesser animal or another bird who had snatched the chick he might have felt differently but he could not reproach himself over losing to a human. Years of experience had resigned him to the aggressive stupidity but superior strength of humans.

But the attack had unsettled him. He realised how vulnerable his choice of nest was. He was even more on the look-out, wary of the slightest movement. The white Range Rover was wandering along the dusty track towards the south of the island beside the fish-filled lochans, but too far away to be a threat to the eagles.

'Don't you think it's beautiful?' Howard gazed through the windscreen.

Beverly searched for the right words. 'I love the colours of the heather and the flowers. But it still strikes me as being bleak.'

Carl was much more enthusiastic. 'I think the amount of open space is amazing. The beaches with nobody on them.' He suddenly remembered meeting Andrew. 'Well, almost nobody, and the hills.'

'Can we go home soon?' Donna said from the back seat, where she sat huddled in her anorak gazing out at the alien world and resenting every moment she was forced to spend in it.

'I need to get some gas,' said Howard pulling off the road in front of MacBratney's garage, which consisted of two pumps and a lean-to workshop surrounded by vehicles in various stages of disrepair. Howard and Carl jumped out.

Mr MacBratney came towards them, wiping the oil off his hands with some cotton-waste. He recognised his customers immediately but decided to be unimpressed. 'Good day.'

'Could you fill her up, please?'

'Certainly,' Mr MacBratney murmured as he removed the filler cap and inserted the nozzle.

'You don't have lead-free gas out here?' Howard was trying to make conversation.

'I only have two pumps. One for petrol, one for diesel. You are the first person who has ever mentioned the lead-free. Mind you, we have less pollution here of most other kinds and the number of vehicles on the island would hardly seem likely to change that, even allowing for the summer visitors.'

'I guess that's right. Mind you, it is amazing how many times you have to pull off the road to let people pass.'

MacBratney considered that for a moment. 'You don't

*have* to pull off. The tourists soon take fright if you drive straight at them! I've seen some that reverse back to a passing place faster than they drive forwards!'

Howard smiled. 'I guess what you could do with is a wider road and it would be better if they were all tarmac instead of some of these sand tracks.'

Mr MacBratney looked carefully at the Laird. 'Would you have me going out of business? It's broken springs and wrecked suspensions that put the meat on my dinner table.'

Howard could not help laughing. 'I guess you're right but with more lorries on the island the pounding they'd give the roads could soon make them unusable.'

'Are we expecting more lorries then?'

Howard shrugged. 'You never know!'

Shona sat, soaking up the sunshine, in the corner of the hay field nearest the lane, listening to the swish of the scythes and the rattling protest of the corncrakes, angry at having their feeding grounds disturbed by the harvest.

'Keep up!' her father kept calling over his shoulder to Andrew and Sandy as they dropped behind. They were turning over, with long handled, wide tined rakes, the neat rows of cut grass and clover to help it dry more quickly in the heat of the sun.

As the work progressed, the lush grass was steadily cropped and the field took on a neat, well-combed look. For Shona it served as a reminder of the brief nature of the island summer, for this hay would be used to provide feed for the animals during the long winter days, which drew nearer with every swish of the blade.

'Lunch time!' Mother called out to the men as she settled a wicker basket down beside Shona.

Mrs MacLeod spread out a flour sack, white from frequent washing and blanched by drying in the sun, and laid out a pat of pale yellow butter, a hunk of cheese, both made from Morag's milk, together with a freshly baked girdle scone and a home-made mutton pie. There was a bottle of her own nettle beer for Shona's father, home-made ginger beer for Shona and a bottle of shop bought lemonade for the boys.

'Shona, you'll need to go down to the shop after you've had your food, for some more of this poison for your brothers.' Andrew and Sandy grinned at each other. 'You've acquired some curious tastes since you've been schooling on the mainland, and that's a fact.'

Shona nodded. Her mouth was too full of melting butter and warm crumbs of girdle scone to attempt a reply.

'Who's this now?' her father enquired, stretching his neck to get a better view of a vehicle that was groaning towards them.

It was an old, bull-nosed Morris Traveller. The green paintwork had been attacked by years of exposure to the salt of the sea air which was also causing the varnish to peel off the woodwork that ran beneath the windows and separated its metal panels.

'It's the doctor, who else?' Mrs MacLeod beamed. At their house Dr MacGregor was always welcome.

The car stopped with a squeal of brakes and the large man heaved himself out.

'It's a fine day! And you all ought to be ashamed of yourselves!' Dr MacGregor was in his shirt sleeves.

Mr MacLeod gave him a wry look. 'Oh, and why is that?'

'Why?' said the Doctor with a perfectly straight face. 'I would have thought you could have found better things to do with your time on a day like this than lie around in the fields. Have you no work to do?'

Mrs MacLeod smiled. 'I sometimes think you can smell my mutton pie from the other end of the island. Would you care for a small piece?'

The Doctor swung himself over the fence and sat down beside Shona. 'Well, not *too* small a piece, Mrs MacLeod. I've come a long way for this, as you said. I was attending Donald MacLeish's wife, who's about to have a baby any second, when I got a whiff of your pie and I told her straight she'd have to postpone the birth at least until the afternoon as I had pressing business at the MacLeods'.'

74

They all smiled at the Doctor. He was nearing seventy, showed all the energy and humour of a much younger man and seemed to have no inclination to retire. An ex-ship's doctor, he had settled on the island at the end of the war saying that whilst he loved the sea he preferred vessels which did not move around on it. He treated the whole island as a ship and its inhabitants as the crew which was why he had no hesitation in discussing patients' ailments, believing them to be common knowledge, with anyone. Yet nobody could keep a secret better than the old doctor, when he believed it necessary.

'Would you care for some nettle beer, Doctor?' Mrs MacLeod asked, taking the bottle from her husband.

Mr MacLeod half-rose. 'I've a flask of whisky in the house.'

The Doctor waved him down again, polishing the neck of the beer bottle with his hand. 'Whisky is best kept for medicinal purposes. I usually have a dram after a night call.' He took a swig from the bottle and handed it back. 'Have you seen much of your neighbours lately?'

Shona, knowing he could only mean the Angus brothers, pricked up her ears.

'The less I see of them, the better I like it,' said Mr MacLeod.

'I tend to share your feelings but I ran up against Red Angus last night making his way down to the ferry. I was called out to the hotel, one of the visitors had eaten a lobster that appeared to have died from old age, and on my way back I almost knocked Red Angus down. Mind you, he was in such a state he looked as if somebody had already tried.'

'Aye? I've not set eyes on the pair of them for days.'

'Blood was coming from his hands and his face. He was in a bad way, so bad that I stopped to offer him some first aid but he wasn't having any.'

'Had he been drinking?'

'Smelled like a distillery! Although I think, for once, that was a good thing. If it hadn't been for the anaesthetic effect of the whisky I think he would have been in considerable pain.'

'Had he been in a fight, do you think?'

Shona could hardly wait for the answer.

'That's what I wondered until I got closer but then it looked more as if he had been attacked by an animal than a human.'

Mr MacLeod shook his head. 'Whatever it was it would no doubt have had good reason.'

The Doctor nodded. 'Wouldn't let me lay a finger on him. Muttered something about not missing the ferry and rushed off into the night.' He turned to Andrew. 'Speaking of fighting, I hear you're turning into something of a pugilist, young man.'

Andrew flushed crimson.

'Word travels fast on the island,' Mrs MacLeod said through pursed lips. 'It's a shame people don't put put more energy into their own affairs rather than other people's.'

'Ah, now, Mrs MacLeod, this was not idle gossip. I happened to be up at the Big House.'

Shona glanced up sharply. She thought of Carl being permanently injured by Andrew's devastating blow.

The Doctor turned to Andrew. 'It seems to me you made a big impression on the Laird's son.'

Anxiously Mrs MacLeod asked, 'Was that why you were at the Big House?'

Doctor MacGregor shook his head. 'Nothing so interesting, I fear. I don't think Andrew damaged anything other than that young man's pride. No, it was the daughter I went to see, to treat a hypothetical case of sinusitis.'

Mrs MacLeod, always interested in medical matters, asked, 'And what would you prescribe for that, Doctor?'

'I would like to have put her across my knee to see if that improved her condition. It's not a cure normally found in medical books and I did not prescribe it in case my colleagues at the British Medical Association disapproved.'

Mrs MacLeod could not resist a smile. The Doctor, who could be the kindest, most patient man in the world, did not suffer timewasters gladly.

'I gave her some of my efficacious pills.'

'Effie who?' asked Sandy.

'Sugar pills,' Doctor MacGregor explained. 'They taste pleasant. I dye them several different colours in case the patient finds that one kind works better than another. People have been known to recover from the most amazing illnesses after taking them.' Doctor MacGregor smiled at the look of astonishment on the children's faces as he revealed his secret. 'The only reason I'm telling you about them is because I never have to prescribe them for islanders.' He beamed down, over the tops of his half-rimmed glasses at Shona. 'And how's my favourite ex-patient?'

Shona always made a special effort for him and put on a lop-sided smile. 'F. .F. .ine. .r,' she got out, almost in a whisper.

He held out his hand to her. He waited without seeming the least impatient while it took her three tries to put her hand into his. That was why she was never flustered with him. He made the time to wait and was never embarrassed by her failures.

His hand was so much softer than her parents' work-worn hands and, despite the warmth of the day, the fingers were cool. Shona remembered his hand stroking her brow when she was little and had a fever. He eased the heat and pain out of her head far more quickly than any medicine he gave her.

'I often think back, young lady, to the day you were born. You looked like a skinned rabbit. Do you know that?' Shona nodded, he had said it to her a thousand times. 'I never thought you would grow into the fine, young lady you have.'

For one fleeting moment Shona felt that she had become the person he was describing. He had always had that kind of power over her but as she had grown older and realised her true limitations even the Doctor's magic had seemed to become weaker. The feeling of being 'a fine, young lady' quickly ebbed away and she returned to being the weak, uncoordinated girl that she was.

He must have read that in her eyes, for a cloud passed across his face and he turned towards her mother. 'She'll be going to the mainland with the boys after the summer holidays?'

Shona sensed the cloud spreading over all of them as she realised, probably for the first time, how little she wanted to leave her mother and the island. It was also easy to see from the expressions on the boys' faces that they were not relishing the prospect either.

Despite the warmth of the sun, she shivered and took her hand away from the Doctor's.

'We must wait and see,' her mother said softly. 'We've made no plans about that yet. Shona, remember you must go down to Mr Mackay's. There's a few things we need.'

The Doctor jumped up, anxious to make amends for his tactlessness. 'It's on my way, I'll drop you off, Shona.'

Shona enjoyed bumping along the track sitting in the front seat of the Doctor's car. Her usual surroundings seemed so unreal when she looked at them through the windows. Her parents had no car and she rarely rode in one, and sometimes the unfamiliar sensation of movement confused her senses so that she believed that it was the car that was stationary and the world which rushed past her.

They paused to let a tourist's car pass at the junction where the track met the narrow, tarmac road which ran down the middle of the island.

'Seal!' the Doctor growled through his teeth whilst managing at the same time to wave and smile at the driver who thought him friendly and waved back. Shona giggled.

Several times along the road, which was so narrow two cars could not pass on it, the Doctor courteously pulled off into a passing place to let another driver through. Every time he smiled and hissed abuse between his teeth.

At last he pulled on to the gravel forecourt of Mr MacKay's shop. It was a long, low building built of whitewashed breeze-block. The few windows it had were placed just below the pink, asbestos-tiled roof and they were long and thin, more like letter boxes than windows.

The shop door had no glass but was solid wood and painted dark green. Above the door was a sign which said 'MacKay, Grocers, Drapers and General Merchants. Established 1803.'

Dr MacGregor leant across to open the door for Shona, managing to give the impression he was doing it only out of courtesy and not because she could not manage it perfectly well for herself.

'Have a good holiday, young Shona!'

She tried to reply, but this time the words would not come. Instead she nodded, smiled and stroked his arm.

He closed the door after her and sat watching Shona's uncertain progress towards the shop. Lately he could not keep from wondering about some of the decisions they had made about her all those years ago.

As she disappeared through the shop doorway he threw the car into gear with a clang and pulled out sharply on to the road, narrowly missing a white Range Rover.

'Seal!' he growled, but this time he did not smile.

In MacKay's store you could buy everything from a pound of tea or a pin, to a litre of paraffin. The goods for sale were piled unceremoniously on bare, unpainted wooden shelves supported by metal frames in tiers of four that rose from floor to ceiling. They ran not only round the outer walls but in a double row, back to back, down the centre of the store.

Very little light came through the tiny windows and the naked fluorescent tubes, high up under the roof, burned even during the brightest day.

When Shona walked in Mr MacKay was deep in conversation with Mrs MacBratney, the tall, thin wife of the island's garage mechanic.

'Hello, Shona,' he called out.

Shona nodded at him and offered the list her mother had sent, not trusting her daughter to select the goods for herself and knowing Shona would be unable to ask for them.

'I'll see to you in just a minute, Shona, when I've finished with Mrs MacBratney.'

Mrs MacBratney appeared to smile vaguely at something invisible dangling above Shona's head. Shona was used to people who avoided looking directly at her.

'Why don't you have a look round, my dear?' Mr MacKay suggested from behind the pile of cardboard boxes, full of sweets and chocolates, which were stuffed on to an old rickety kitchen table. The table also held an old, brass cash register that still calculated in pounds, shillings and pence.

Shona, like all the locals, did not need to 'look round'. She knew from habit where everything lived though the order had been established, without any kind of logic, almost as long as the family had run the store. Cornflakes rested cheek by jowl with corn plasters without anyone realising they both happened to begin with the letter 'C'!

Locals were perfectly content with the system and tourists, though more confused, were happy to regard it as quaint. The store's huge stock of such a diverse range of goods might have seemed odd to the summer visitors but it proved an enormous comfort to the locals when the island was cut off for weeks at a time during the winter gales.

The main reason for Mr MacKay's invitation to wander round the store was so that he could continue his gossip with Mrs MacBratney and the first words Shona overheard made certain that her ears remained well tuned to the conversation.

'The Laird said that he wants to put up a new building,' said Mr MacKay.

Mrs MacBratney was clearly shocked. 'But you've only had this place these last twenty years. I mind well the time your mother ran the store in the best parlour up at your house.'

'Aye, well, he thinks I need refrigerated display cabinets, like they have on the mainland and that I should have a big, huge window all down that side.'

'Whatever for?'

'So that people can see it's a shop, he said.'

'But everybody *knows* it's a shop. It's the only one on the island.'

Mr MacKay nodded. 'He thinks it ought to *look* like one though. Which is why he wants to put in this fine big window.'

'And the first winter gale will take it straight out again!' Mrs MacBratney said scornfully.

Mr MacKay nodded in agreement. 'And the cost! He's no doubt trying to find a way of putting up my rent, that's all. I suspect he'll have second thoughts when he realises that everything has to come from the mainland and costs three times as much by the time it lands here. And when Fergus called with the mails this morning he tells me the Laird's been talking about building a great factory for processing fish and seaweed over on the west side of the island.'

'But the boats would never get in there, it's far too shallow!'

'Fergus says the Laird intends dredging it. But then, I says, how's he going to get the stuff out to the ferry with nothing but a sandy track, fit only for a horse and cart, between the west side and the quay?'

'Ah,' it was Mrs MacBratney's turn to sound knowing, 'have you not heard about all the new, good, wide roads he's going to build? He mentioned to my husband when he called to buy petrol.'

'We've heard it all before! These people come up here with their grand plans to change the world but they lose interest quickly enough in my experience.' Mr MacKay shook his head.

Shona hoped they would lose interest. She wanted her island to stay the way it was. Nothing she had heard so far sounded like a change for the better.

The shop bell rang out and Mrs Taggart, the mother of the girl who had once pushed Shona over and incurred Andrew's wrath, came in through the door.

Shona sighed knowing that they would now have to bring *her* up to date with the rumours before she got served.

'And that's not the worst,' said Mrs Taggart when they had finished, 'have you not heard about the two metre high electric fence he's going to put across the island to keep in the deer?'

# Nine

Shona woke in the middle of the night to hear what sounded like two cows calling to each other.

She rolled on her side and lay very still to listen properly. The sounds came again and she was able to identify them at once. The deeper sound, the one like the mother cow, was the fog-horn from the lighthouse which was set on a jagged outcrop of rock off the southernmost point of the island. The lighter, hoarser sound, which could easily have been its lost calf, was the answering call of a small ship, feeling its way blind along the channel whilst trying to warn other ships of its approach.

They were desolate sounds which filled Shona with dread ever since the days when she used to listen anxiously for the safe return of Uncle James's fishing boat. She always believed she would recognise the distinctive note of his boat's compressed air fog-horn but, like tonight, when the moment came all the fog-horns sounded alike.

Sometimes there would be several boats, each bleakly warning the others of their presence. Shona concentrated so hard she almost stopped breathing, particularly if she believed they were drawing closer either to each other or, to her and the shore. Although the western coast was composed mainly of long sandy beaches not far from the shore there were, just beneath the surface, vast ribs of rock which could easily rip the bottom out of a ship.

Shona derived no comfort from the fact that Uncle James, like a good many islanders and particularly fishermen, could not swim. Both the main reasons for this were thought to be practical. Firstly, few learnt because for most of the year the temperature of the waters surrounding the island would deter any but the extremely hardy, or the foolhardy, from entering them and secondly, many fishermen believed that if they were going to drown the sooner it was over the better.

Only recently, since the children had gone to the mainland school, equipped with heated, indoor pools, had islanders learnt to swim and many there were who saw that more as another interference in the traditional life of the island rather than as a step forward.

But tonight the little ship disappeared safely into the distance and Shona eventually fell asleep, counting off, like sheep, the seconds of silence between the regular eruptions from the lighthouse.

The eaglets were cold, damp and hungry. Their parents too were dull-eyed and bedraggled, hunched round the nest, grounded by the dispiriting fog. The male stretched his wings as if he might launch into a glide but he was only trying to shake the glistening pearls of damp from his feathers. He knew only too well that nothing would stir far today. Smaller animals would stay curled in the dry warmth of their nests and burrows. There was no point in wasting what little energy he had trying to hunt.

The female arched her wings over the nest to keep the damp off the eaglets but it was hardly necessary. They were almost fully fledged and very soon her long weeks at the nest would be over. Soon they would try out their wings, learn to fly and eventually hunt for themselves.

She still had doubts that the weaker of the two would fly. It was getting less and less of its fair share of the food. If it got much weaker the stronger one might tip it out of the nest while her back was turned.

She stretched her neck and settled it down against her back, gazing patiently at the fog.

*

'But I need that coach-house work finishing by the end of the week, MacPherson.' Howard knew it had been a mistake to let the guy hire just anybody! 'What's the hold up?'

'They need plasterboard and planking.'

'So? Go out and buy the stuff!'

'It had to be ordered from the mainland, Mr Kleinberger, and should have been over on the ferry but the fog was so thick it did not sail again last night.'

'I've got two highly paid guys sitting on their butts waiting to install the computers. How are the circuits?'

Mr MacPherson, who understood land but was easily defeated by technology, looked puzzled. 'I beg your pardon?'

'The electricity and telecommunications circuits.'

'The electrics are finished and the man from British Telecom is also waiting for the ferry to run again.'

'The other day when we were driving round the island I noticed the telegraph poles but there were no wires running between them.'

Mr MacPherson smiled. 'Ah, yes. The cables were so often blown down in the winter gales that they took them down and buried them beneath the ground.'

Relieved, Howard nodded and then looked puzzled again. 'So why leave the poles if they don't carry anything?'

'They are for the birds.' MacPherson could see he was still not getting through. 'There are very few trees on the island, except for your own plantation, and the poles were left so that owls and hawks have somewhere to perch.'

Howard could hardly believe his ears. If he had not known what a humourless man MacPherson was he would have thought the Factor was having him on. For the birds! Sometimes he thought the whole island was strictly for the birds! Out loud he said, 'Does this happen often? I mean the ferry not running.'

'That would depend on what you mean by "often". It usually happens more frequently during the storms in the winter. Apart from fresh food, it's mostly a question of planning ahead. Had we known what you intended to do we could have got the materials here in advance and there need have been no delay.'

Howard sighed. 'You're right, MacPherson, it's my own fault. To tell the truth I hadn't intended having a set-up like this at all up here. I thought I could manage with just the telephone but it hasn't worked out like that. I feel more cut off from my office than I expected.' He passed a hand wearily across his forehead. 'I had hoped that the time up here could be some sort of sabbatical, a holiday, but I've worked every day of my life. When I was a kid I used to sell papers on the street corner and even when I was in Grade School I always had a job. I don't find it easy to stop.'

'I had noticed, sir.'

Howard grinned. 'Been driving you a bit hard with all my plans and propositions, have I?'

MacPherson shook his head. 'Believe me, we are all pleased that anybody should take such a personal interest in the island. It is a long time since anybody thought of it as anything but a piece of what I think you call "real estate".'

'I think this island is a real beautiful place and without destroying the life it's got I want to make sure it can carry on long after you and I are gone. I don't want to make changes for change's sake but if things stay just as they are there'll only be old people living here in fifty years' time. I don't want to make a profit out of the place but it isn't in my nature to let it run at a loss. I'd be content if it could break even. Besides, it needs work to keep the young people here.'

MacPherson nodded. 'That's perfectly true. The only thing I would say, if you'll allow me . . . ?' Howard nodded. 'The islanders have lived without hope of change for a good many years now. I would be careful of raising their expectations too high, making promises you cannot keep.'

'I understand that.'

'Rumours are flying round the island. Just at the minute the arrival of a rocket launching pad would not surprise them.'

'I think I can spare them Cape Canaveral.'

'It's just that people are apt to pick up on the slightest thing you say at the moment.'

'You think I shouldn't *talk* to them?'

'To give you an example. The other day you called for some petrol at Mr MacBratney's. You happened to mention something about the roads being narrow.'

'I was just passing the time of day, making conversation, if you will.'

'I'm sure you meant no harm, but by the *end* of that day word was going round the island that you intended to rebuild and widen all the existing roads, not to mention adding a few new ones.'

'I said no such thing!'

'I'm perfectly certain you didn't, but do you see what I mean? The spark is already there, waiting to be fuelled.'

'I take your point. Thanks for warning me. I'll be more careful. One thing we did discuss that I would like to go ahead with is expanding the deer stalking. There are people in Europe who would pay a fortune to take part in that.'

'Do you mean shoots?'

'Only when we need to cull the old and weak stock, and we'd charge extra for those. But stalking itself is big business if you can let the right people know it's available. I'll get my London office to do some research on where we should advertise and check with Hamish MacDonald, at the hotel, about spare rooms.'

'I think he always has a few.'

'I mean for party bookings. When's the best time? We don't want to clash with a time when he's already got plenty of visitors if we can get people to come when he's a bit slack.'

'I'll get on to it straight away. By the way, Henderson . . .' Howard looked puzzled, '. . . the one who looks after the deer, said he thought somebody was up there the other day.'

'Tourists? How did he know?'

'He was coming back from his rounds when he heard a great commotion up by the golden eagle's nest. He wondered if somebody was up there after the deer.'

'Poachers?'

'They usually only go after rabbits for the pot. There are those who take some trout or the odd salmon but unless it gets out of hand we normally turn a blind eye.'

'Taking deer would be a whole different ball game.'

'Well, Henderson will keep his eyes open but he cannot be everywhere at once.'

Howard looked thoughtful. 'Maybe we should reconsider the idea we discussed about a fence.'

'I hope it won't come to that. It would be very expensive.'

'And an eyesore!'

'It's a bad thing we got the hay cut just before this came down on us,' Mr MacLeod said, gazing out at the thick fog swirling round the croft. 'All the goodness will leach out of it lying in this wet.'

Mrs MacLeod, the only one with work to do when the weather was bad, looked up from her baking. 'Maybe there'll be a wind that clears the fog away and some sun to dry the hay.' There were shouts from the boys' room. 'What are those two up to now? They can't be alone for five minutes without falling out.'

Shona, who had been with them for a while but grown tired of their quarrels, sat on the sofa beneath the window which dripped condensation from the fine heat Mrs MacLeod had stoked up for the baking.

She would love to have been up to her elbows in flour like her mother but she knew better than to get under foot. Sometimes towards the end of a session she might be allowed to twist waste pastry into weird shapes, which Shona believed were rabbits, pushing in currants for eyes. Until then there was nothing to do but wait.

'I thought we might be cutting the peat by now.' Mr MacLeod, having so much work on his hands hated the enforced idleness every bit as much as Shona. 'We'll have to wait for that to dry too now.'

'It's early in the year yet.' Mrs MacLeod was used to her

husband's black moods when things were not as he wanted them.

'Oh yes, and before we know the sheep shearing will be upon us.' He paused for a moment before he added, 'Maybe for the last time too!'

'Och, I've not patience with you when you talk like that. Mr MacPherson was only trying to frighten us with that talk about the land. Of course, he'll renew the lease on the hillside.'

'You are just guessing, woman! You have no more idea of what's in their minds than I do.'

Mrs MacLeod impatiently banged the rolling pin down on the table sending a cloud of flour into the air.

Shona hated arguments of any kind. When they happened, particularly between people she loved, something inside her seemed to shrivel. She slid quietly off the sofa and lifted her black oilskin off the hook on the back of the door.

'And where's she off to?' Mr MacLeod demanded.

Shona shrugged.

'Leave the girl alone,' her mother said quietly. 'She can go for a walk if she wants to, can't she?'

Mr MacLeod looked outraged, as if Shona had announced her intention to walk barefoot across hot coals. 'In this?' If he was stuck indoors he could not understand anyone else wanting to be outside.

'And why not? I've got to listen to you moaning away but she does not.' She broke off to turn to Shona. 'Take care, don't be outside too long.'

Shona smiled and went out into the air which felt even colder than she expected after the enveloping heat of the kitchen. As she passed the window she heard her father growling, 'It isn't safe for her to be wandering about out there in this weather.'

'Don't be telling me. Isn't it you that drove her out, just, with your grumbling?'

Shona hurried away and heard no more.

'I'd like my whole bedroom to be yellow.' Donna dumped a

pile of paint sample cards down on the table in front of her mother who was busy looking through swatches of curtain materials which she had received through the post before the ferry stopped. 'This is my favourite, Southern Sun.'

Beverly looked over her glasses, which she hated wearing but needed for close work and reading. 'Mmm, that's a lovely colour and there's some material that would go with it for drapes and maybe a bed cover.' She turned over one of the swatches to reveal a contrasting shade of yellow in a plain cotton.

'Not cotton!' Donna exploded. 'I thought of velvet.'

'Velvet would cost a fortune on those huge windows.'

Carl tried to close his ears. Perfectly happy with his own room as it was he could think of nothing more boring than yet another discussion, which would no doubt quickly turn into an argument with Donna stamping off in a rage, about how she wanted her room.

She had already got Flora and Donald to move all the furniture out of her room, including the carpet, and had then got Donald to paint the floorboards in an unbelievable shade of orange.

It was a shade Mr MacKay had had sitting on the shelf for several years since the only people who had ever used a can said the colour made them feel bilious.

Donna was currently sleeping on the bare boards with just a mattress and a duvet, awaiting the arrival from London of the new, matt-black bedroom furniture and lime green carpet she had persuaded her long-suffering father to order. She had even wanted to manage without the mattress, saying it gave her bad dreams sleeping on something other people had used, but her father drew the line at that!

'If I can't have velvet I'd rather have nothing at all.'

'Donna, be reasonable, honey!' To Carl that seemed like asking the impossible of his sister. 'You'll need something just to keep out the cold.'

'And velvet will keep out more than cotton,' Donna said triumphantly.

Carl was used to Donna getting her own way. It did not really bother him, he just did not enjoy listening to the whole gruesome process.

Beverly swung round. 'Carl, where are you going?'

'Just for a walk.'

'In that?' Beverly pointed at the fog through the window with her spectacle frames.

'He's nuts,' Donna dismissed him, hating to be deflected from the argument she was having, especially as she was winning.

'I won't be gone long, honest, Mom.'

'But I thought we should choose some drapes for your room.'

Carl shrugged, anxious to get out. 'I'm happy with what I've got.'

'He doesn't mind living amongst trash!' Donna said scornfully.

'No, Donna. What I don't like,' Carl spoke carefully, 'are people who are never content with what they've got and scream when they don't get their own way.'

Donna flushed with anger. 'You've no right to say that!'

But Carl had closed the door and gone.

Shona had wandered down to the beach. It was cold and grey surrounded by the thick fog. The lighthouse fog-horn was still giving off its regular blasts and though she expected them, each time they made her jump, they seemed so loud.

The fog reminded her of the stories her uncle used to tell of mermaids who would appear to sailors during the thickest of fogs and lure them to their doom on strands of rock.

There were also stories of ghost ships which sounded their fog-horns only to confuse honest captains who would, by trying to avoid collision with the non-existent ghost ship, set a course which led to their own destruction. What made these stories so especially cruel, Shona felt, was that the ghost ships were supposedly crewed by long dead sailors and fishermen who had themselves been sent to their doom by other ghost ships.

Shona shivered as she looked at the cold, grey edges of the sea which slopped about under the wet folds of fog. She stomped off along the beach deserted but for a few grounded gulls. They looked bored as they poked about in the sand searching for lug worms, like holidaymakers trying to make the best of things until the weather improved.

She had wandered, slowly stopping to poke about in pools, almost to the far end of the beach before she realised it. With the fog blotting out the view she had not noticed she had come so far. She was about to turn for home when she saw something orange moving about in the mist where an outcrop of rocks and some quicksand separated her bay from the next.

Her head full of ghost ships and treacherous mermaids she edged forward peering into the wreaths of mist.

At first she thought she must have imagined it, there was nothing to see. But then the mist thinned and the orange thing was there again.

Trying to keep it in sight and yet not stumble she moved forward as quickly and quietly as she dared. She did not want to frighten it away, whatever it was, but also she did not want it to see her. At least, not until she knew exactly what kind of an *it* it was, lurking in the fog.

She managed to establish it was moving away and not towards her, which was a comfort because unless she made a sound, or the thing had eyes in the back of its head, she was unlikely to be spotted. But she was taking no chances. When she reached the end of the sands and began to clamber over the jagged rocks she slowed down to snail's pace for fear of dislodging a stone and attracting the thing's attention.

But suddenly the thing disappeared from view. It had completely vanished. There was no sign of anything moving in the mist ahead of her, orange or otherwise, and no sound, but for the distant swish of the sea and the monotonous blasts from the lighthouse.

Bit by bit Shona eased forward but whatever apparition it was she had seen had disappeared without trace.

'Oh, no! It's you!'

Shona almost died of shock! She swung round and through the mist discovered that her orange sprite was Carl.

Realising, by some sixth sense, that he was being followed he had pressed himself back into a fissure in the rock while whoever it was caught up with him.

'You're the MacLeod girl, aren't you? The one who got me into trouble the other day.'

Shona, powerless to answer him, just stood.

'It was your brother who attacked me up in the sand-dune.'

Allowing for a little exaggeration what he said was true, she only wished it was not.

'Don't just stand there, say something for Heaven's sakes!' Carl, wrong-footed by the girl's refusal to speak, pulled off his misted up glasses and polished them furiously. When, by the time he had replaced them, she still had not spoken he lost all patience with her. 'Clear off and leave me in peace. I'm not doing you any harm, so there's no need to set your brothers on me today.'

As he turned his back on her and continued scrambling over the rocks to get to the next bay Shona sank down on to a boulder.

The unfamiliar pricking in the corners of her eyes were tears. Angrily, with the backs of her fists, she rubbed them away. How could he be so cruel? He had no right to make her cry! But then perhaps he was not to blame. His attitude showed just how much things had changed, and all for the worse, since the evening when she had seen him arrive on the quay with his family.

He had all but been swallowed up by the fog. Shona was left with her own thoughts and the constant bleating of the fog-horn. And then she realised he was heading for the quicksand.

She pulled herself up. She must stop him. As she blundered after him across the sharp, uneven surface of the rock she tried to shout a warning. 'Ar---ee--gath!'

Her first attempt was lost, drowned out by the fog-horn. The second was better timed. He heard her.

'Go away! Leave me alone!'

Unable to understand what Shona was saying he must have kept on going because although she was moving quite quickly she could see no sign of him.

Concentrate, she told herself, try to get your brain and your lips together, just this once, or he's going to die!

But it was not easy to concentrate on the mechanics of a mouth whilst careering across the rocks, trying not to fall. Perhaps if she stopped, tried to do one thing at a time.

'Qw . . e . k.' She had managed that bit, but the second part of the word refused to come out. Instead her lips writhed soundlessly until a trail of spittle ran down her chin.

Whether he heard her or not she did not know, he certainly did not bother to reply.

If only she could get hold of him she would *make* him listen!

Suddenly the rocks seemed to drop away beneath her feet. She had reached the slope which led down to another, apparently perfectly ordinary, beach.

And there he was. Just below her, about to step off the rocks on to innocent-looking sand which would swallow him alive in seconds.

There was no more time to waste shouting at him. He refused to take any notice and could not understand a word she was trying to say.

She looked round, picked up the largest lump of rock she could find, prayed that her sense of direction and strength would be better than usual, and hurled it down.

It whistled past Carl's ear. 'Hey, what the hell? You *are* crazy!'

Then he realised that she was pointing at something beyond him. At the beach. He turned back just in time to see the rock disappearing beneath the shifting surface of the quicksand.

He sat down abruptly, as if the stone had felled him. 'Jeeez!'

# Ten

Shona, mentally and physically exhausted, stood at the top of the rocks motionless, pale and wreathed in fog, as if she were carved out of granite.

Below her Carl crouched on his boulder, his whole body shaking uncontrollably. One more step and he would have been up to his armpits in the quicksand, sinking rapidly to a suffocating death. He could almost taste the sand forcing its way into his nose and mouth; feel it cramming its ooze into his eyes and ears.

A small, muddy bubble on the surface of the diabolically innocent looking sand was the only evidence that the rock, which the MacLeod girl had thrown as a warning, had ever existed. Whether it was still sinking or had come to rest two or six metres beneath the surface was a subject Carl could not bring himself to think about.

Slowly Carl began to recover. He got up and turned to face the girl. To his surprise he could see, even through the mist, that she was crying. There was no sound, no movement of her thin shoulders, but tears, of shock presumably, were trickling down her cheeks.

Instantly, his own feelings forgotten, he was bounding up the rocks towards her.

Not knowing what he intended she flinched when he got close. He grabbed her shoulders, putting his face up close to hers. 'It's OK. Hey, come on! I'm all right. There's no need to cry.'

She turned away. He let go of her shoulders, embarrassed at touching her.

He was not used to touching girls, even his own sister. *Especially* his own sister! Donna hated to be touched and only grudgingly allowed her father to hug her after she had graciously consented to accept yet another gift.

'Hey, thanks for what you did. After everything that happened the other day and all . . .' Carl's voice trailed away.

He knew that what he had said was, in the circumstances, inadequate but felt that actually to mention saving his life would sound about as sincere as an acceptance speech for an Oscar. Besides, saying it out loud meant bringing out into the open something he was already trying to put out of his mind for ever. Once it was said out loud they might even have to *discuss* it!

He was relieved when she did not seem to expect more from him but puzzled that all she did was shake her head, a little uncertainly, from side to side.

He tried to move the conversation on.

'My name's Carl, but I guess you already know that.'

He paused, expecting her to reply. He was used to conversation being like tennis. He had sent down a good serve, but she had ignored it.

Second service, he thought. 'What's your name? I know you're a MacLeod, but what do they call you? I mean, your first name, what's that?'

The girl flushed but still did not answer.

Carl, thinking that he had at long last hit on somebody as awkward as himself perked up. 'Hey, let me guess! Jeannie?'

She smiled and shook her head.

Carl thought her red-gold hair, even dampened by the mist, was a much neater shade than her brothers' garish red. 'Mary?'

Again she shook her head.

'Flora? Liz? Angie? Cora Beth?'

Suddenly the girl, having done nothing but shake her head, threw back her head and laughed.

The laugh jolted Carl. It was somewhere between a nail being scraped across glass and a rusty hinge.

But so what? Lots of girls have crazy laughs, he thought, though he could not name one and trying drove any other names out of his head. 'I give up. You'll have to tell me.'

Her face was serious again now. Wasn't this one of the reasons she avoided the tourists? Everyone on the island knew her name, her family, the people at school, she had never had to say it, did not imagine that she could.

'Come on!' Carl urged. 'The suspense is killing me!'

She concentrated very hard, trying to shape her lips so that they would make the sound that was crystal clear inside her head.

Carl went very cold. He thought she looked as if she was going to kiss him!

'Shhh . . .'

She had managed to get out the first bit. Painstakingly she rearranged her lips into the shape of the next sound. She remembered her mother, whilst trying to teach her how to talk, had said it was like blowing a bubble. Not that she had ever succeeded in blowing one.

'Oh . . .' The effort she was having to put into this simple act of saying her own name was incredible and the worst was yet to come.

Carl did not know where to look. He could not work out exactly what her problem was, merely that she had one and he could only assume that watching her made it worse. It certainly did for him! But to look away seemed incredibly rude.

He desperately wanted to help but there was nothing he could do. He had tried to guess her name and failed. He could not think of a single name that began with 'Show', if that was what she was trying to say. The only alternative he had left was to look her steadily in the eyes and wait. It seemed like forever!

'Maa,' she said and before she could correct herself Carl had picked it up and run with it.

'Shoma. What an unusual name. I never heard that before.

I guess it's Scottish. I learnt to say "Scottish", my father says you should only use Scotch for the drink.' Carl poured out a torrent of verbal diarrhoea. He would have recited the Constitution of the United States, read the phone book, anything to prevent her having to speak again. His stomach ached with the embarrassment he had just put them both through.

He was so busy talking he did not realise that she was shaking her head, trying to get her name across to him again. He was not looking any more, just talking so as not to be swallowed up by any more of her never-ending pauses which were the oral equivalent of the quicksands he had so recently escaped.

Shona knew only too well what he was doing, it had happened to her so often in the past.

'Would your daughter like a glass of milk?' People often asked her mother, trying to avoid having to wait for Shona to reply.

Very occasionally, and usually only to relatives, her mother would tartly reply, 'I don't know. Why don't you ask her?'

At last Carl simply ran out of words, coloured slightly and began to walk away back up the rocks.

'Come on, let's get out of this place, it gives me the creeps.'

Silently she followed him.

He did not know quite what to do with her. He remembered some kind of Chinese proverb which went something like, if somebody saves your life they *own* you. If that was true, and he could understand the feeling behind it, then he was stuck with her, at least for the rest of the afternoon.

Nor had he noticed, until now, that she walked rather oddly. He had assumed that all that arm waving she'd been doing down on the beach the other day had been some kind of act, put on deliberately to scare off the birds he was watching. Only now did he realise that it was part of her normal, if that was the right word, walk. Perhaps he should not be making her walk? But, awkward as it looked, it did not seem to cause her any pain and it was certainly better than listening to her struggling to talk.

'I've taken up bird-watching,' he said without thinking. As soon as he had spoken he wished that he could swallow the words up again but to his enormous relief she nodded. To Carl it seemed more of a diagonal nod than a straight yes or no but at least it was better than her forcing herself to talk and it took the enormous weight out of the silence which had fallen over them.

'I haven't seen too many yet but I'm keeping a list. That's what I was doing the other day when . . .' Carl's voice trailed away. That was the trouble with doing all the talking, it left spaces into which you put things you had not intended to say.

'I'm sorry, I didn't mean to bring that up.' Again he could have kicked himself. Why did he keep saying things that needed answers?

But Shona let him off the hook again, she simply shrugged a kind of one shoulder shrug without bothering to look at him.

Stupid of him – he should have realised that she'd been living with this problem for a long time and knew the ways round it. It was only when she was forced into the position of having to answer, like saying her name, that she would try. After all you could hardly mime your name!

'Shona, maybe you could go bird-watching with me sometime. Would you like that?'

Her eyes, her whole face, lit up. Carl was taken aback not only by her reaction but by the change it brought over her. She caught his arm, pointed beyond the dunes and tugged at him. Her eyes still had their sparkle but there was something about her face, almost as if she expected him to pull away from her.

Carl felt guilty. In some ways that was exactly what he wanted to do. He felt that their relationship, if you could call it that, had maybe developed enough for one day, but he also felt he could not walk away from somebody who only minutes ago had saved him from almost certain death.

If only she would let go of my arm, he thought and, as if she was a mind reader, she did just that.

'What's up there, birds?' he asked.

Shona nodded.

'But, Shoma, we won't be able to see them through this fog, will we?' She nodded again and he was left with little choice but to follow.

Once they had crossed the dunes and the damp machair they were on quite level ground for some time.

The silence in which they walked felt awkward to Carl. Not that he had anything earth-shattering to say but the odd 'Ouch', or 'Where are we heading?' would have helped him to feel a little easier. He kept having to bite back sentences and slowly he began to realise how carelessly people who, like himself, had no problem with talking, used words and that a great deal of conversation is just talking for talking's sake. Like having a walkman strapped to your head all the time; the noise is to prove to yourself that you exist, that you are not alone in the world.

They not only crossed the sandy track but soon afterwards crossed the main road. Both, because of the weather, were deserted.

It was when the road disappeared in the fog behind them that Carl began to get really nervous.

In the few short days he had been living on the island, apart from the drive round with his parents, the only area he had really explored centred on the house, mostly around the beach. Here he was going off to goodness knows where with a girl who could hardly walk, could not talk properly and whose brother, only a few days back, had physically attacked him!

He could not stop himself wondering if he was behaving sensibly. All the mist and murk, with the constantly bleating fog-horn slowly receding into the distance, did nothing to make him feel any more secure.

Sure, she had just saved his life but what if she was now only leading him into a trap? Perhaps the whole thing was a set-up and she had been sent to lure him off to some remote part of the island where her brother had planned an even more horrible ending for his life.

No, he told himself, that was crazy! Why go to all that trouble? She could have just as easily let him disappear into the quicksand and not tried to stop him. But then the brother would have been deprived of his revenge! Surely it was not enough to know your enemy had died if you were not there to witness the event?

Carl shuddered. He tried to dismiss these as wild thoughts caused by watching too many TV soaps but in this landscape, especially because he could see so little of it, that was not easy.

They seemed to be wandering aimlessly across a wilderness of peat, heather and bracken, skirting a lochan from time to time, and all the girl had to do was abandon him, dodge behind a rock or something, because he knew he would never be able to find his own way back.

It was fortunate that her pace was so slow. At least it was not too difficult to keep up.

But even supposing she was innocent of any dreadful motive, how good was her sense of direction?

He did not really like to think too deeply about the extent of her disabilities. Suppose they did not end with walking and talking? What if she had some serious mental hang-up?

Unfortunately Shona chose that moment to grab his arm.

'Oh!' Carl almost leapt out of his skin. 'I'm sorry . . .' he stopped, she had a finger up to her lips, then suddenly she dropped to her knees.

Oh, my God, he thought, she's going to have a fit!

He was about to help her up, though his first inclination was to run for help, well, to run anyway, when he realised she was crawling forwards on her belly.

If walking was difficult for her, crawling was a good deal worse. Trying to pull herself forwards using only her hands and knees was agonising to watch. Carl stood mesmerized.

She turned to see where he had got to. This she did while balancing on one hand and almost fell over into a clump of heather. When she had recovered she managed to persuade Carl, by urgent gestures, to follow her, which he did at a half crouch.

He caught up with her as the ground began to rise in a low, grassy hillock, She seemed to want to stay behind this mound, as if there was something special on the other side.

This is it, he thought.

Very, very slowly she eased her way forwards and peered round the mound.

Not knowing what to expect, but fearing the worst, he did the same.

They appeared to be on the shore of a loch. How big it was Carl could not tell but it was big enough for the other end to be shrouded in mist, although today that was not saying much. Judging by the complete lack of movement on its flat, black surface it was not a sea loch. There was something unnerving about the perfect, regular curve of its shoreline. It was so perfect that it looked artificial, as if a giant scoop had been used to create it. The grass grew right up to the water's edge with no shingle and no rocks thrusting up out of the water, which made it appear very deep.

But why had she brought him here? Surely they had not come all this way to look at a pool?

Through the mist, from across the pool, came a low, wailing cry.

'What the hell is that?' hissed Carl, forgetting that he was not likely to get a reply.

She pressed hard on his arm and again put her finger to her lips.

How can I be quiet, he wondered, not knowing what on earth is going to come at me out of that mist?

He peered through the gloom until his eyes ached but could make out nothing but the mist curling in wisps off the still, black surface of the water.

Carl jumped as suddenly, up through the calm surface, a large black and white bird appeared. About half a metre long with a long neck, a grey head and a black bill, it had

101

patches of white with black stripes on its back and shoulders which reminded Carl of the American convicts' uniform in old movies.

He had no idea what the bird was and as he had not got his bird book with him there was no way he could identify it but there was something majestic and yet secretive about the bird which made him feel certain he was watching something special.

Carl grinned excitedly at the girl.

She smiled back her lop-sided smile, pleased that she had been able to show him at least one of a pair of birds she had been watching ever since the early spring when they had built their nest and laid the eggs. She had watched the greyish-brown chicks scooting about on the loch. Now they were feeding themselves and soon they would be ready to fly.

Uncle James had first shown her their nesting site, years ago, and the birds had returned to it every year since. Watching them was one of many things she continued to do in the hope that it would make her feel closer to him. Sadly, it usually had the opposite effect.

Today for the first time she had got back something that she believed she might never feel again, the pleasure of sharing.

As they made their way back slowly towards the main road Shona believed that she felt a slight breath of wind, could see further than before, but the fog-horn was still bleating out its warning so she dismissed it.

# Eleven

That night Shona was suddenly woken by the silence. The fog-horn's regular blasts had stopped. It woke her as surely as the stopping of the ticking of a loud clock.

She had not imagined the breeze after all. It must have strengthened and cleared away the fog. She heaved a sigh of relief. She was content with most weather, she could cope with the storms and even snow, but the all-enveloping fog that usually kept the whole family indoors, making her father grumpy because he could not get on with his work, she hated.

Perhaps tomorrow she and Carl could go back and see the whole family of divers on the loch and there were other things too she could show him.

For Shona their chance meeting in the fog seemed to have opened up a whole new way of looking at her life.

There was doubt nagging at the back of her mind. Neither of their families would be very pleased. The fight between Carl and Andrew had soured relationships. Her father had already been threatened with the loss of his extra grazing rights for his sheep, on which the family depended for a living. After that it was difficult to see how they would encourage any kind of friendship between herself and Carl.

There was also the problem of the unwritten rule about incomers. The islanders tended to keep very much to themselves. Experience had shown that to mix with incomers usually only led to grief. This was considered particularly important with tourists. Not that the islanders were anything but polite in their dealings with them, but answering their questions, or helping them if they were lost or in trouble was considered to be the furthest politeness should take them.

Carl was not only an incomer, he was the Laird's son. Shona could not imagine her parents encouraging her to have anything to do with any member of the Laird's family and her father, who had reason to dislike him over the trouble with the grazing, might be very angry indeed.

Shona sighed and rolled over on her pillow. Then it would just have to be a matter that was kept quiet. After all Shona's whole life was a locked-in secret, it would only be one more amongst many.

Hugging herself warm with the glee of that thought Shona drifted gently back to sleep and dreamed of flying high above the island with Carl beside her.

'A black-throated diver!' Carl shouted triumphantly stabbing with his finger the picture of the bird Shona had shown him the previous day.

Flora looked up from the bacon she was frying for herself and Carl; it was too early for the rest of the Kleinberger family to be awake. 'Is that right? Mostly they're just birds to me. Big ones, small ones, brown ones or coloured ones. There are one or two I know well, like the golden eagles, for they're the ones that take and kill the young lambs in the spring.'

'Are there golden eagles on the island too? They're quite rare. Maybe Shoma could point those out to me too, she'll probably know about them.'

Flora looked puzzled. 'Who did you say?'

'Shoma MacLeod, she took me to the loch with the diver on yesterday.'

'That's Shona.'

Carl's toes curled with embarrassment at the memory of having called her by the wrong name all afternoon. 'I thought she said Shoma.' Flora set a plate of eggs and bacon down in front of Carl. 'Thanks, Flora, this looks great. Isn't there any of that black pudding today?'

Flora, tucking into her own food, shook her head. 'There's no more until the ferry comes again, which I expect will be tonight now the fog has lifted.' She deftly wiped egg yolk up from her plate with a corner of bread. 'You say Shona MacLeod was *talking* to you? My – aren't you the honoured one! I've known that poor, wee thing since she was born and I've never heard her utter a single sound, not that you'd really call talking anyway.'

'She wasn't easy to understand, I have to admit. That's why I got her name wrong.'

'That she spoke at all, and you . . .' Flora broke off abruptly and blushed.

Carl grinned. 'It's OK, Flora, you can say it. I know that you call us incomers.'

'Ah, well, that is not what I was going to say at all. I was going to say, and you the Laird's son.'

'So what? Is there any more bacon?'

Flora reached round to the stove and scooped up two more juicy rashers which she dumped on his plate.

'It is not the way things should be, that is all,' she added with a sniff.

'Oh, come on! We're not living in the Middle Ages. Come to that, if talking to Shona is wrong what are we doing sitting here eating breakfast together?'

Flora drew herself up, picked up her empty plate and took it across to the draining board. 'You're quite right, Master Carl.'

'Aw, cut that out, Flora! I hate being called "Master" and besides you and me are friends. I'd rather eat breakfast in here with you than sit in that great empty dining room on my own. We know who we are without me putting on some kind of show. We're all people after all.'

Flora turned the tap on hard. 'There are some that would not see it that way. MacPherson for one.'

'MacPherson's a bit of a stick in the mud!'

'Maybe, but he is the Factor and what he says goes on this island, after your father that is. And what's he going to say about it? Only the other day that Andrew MacLeod knocked you over in a fight and now you are going round the island with his sister!'

Carl looked uncomfortable. 'I'm not going round with her. I happened to meet her, that's all.' He was about to say that she had saved his life by stopping him falling into the quicksand but something, probably the idea that he would look foolish to Flora, prevented him.

'Well, you know your own business best, I suppose.'

Carl thought about that for a moment. 'Well, I won't mention it to anybody else if you won't.'

Flora looked outraged. 'I hope you're not suggesting that I am one for the gossip?'

'I know how stories get around on the island. Nobody in this house mentioned that I'd had a fight with Andrew MacLeod.' Flora banged the dishes in the sink rather louder than was necessary to avoid having to answer.

Carl was just going out through the back door when he stopped and turned back. 'She is OK, isn't she?'

Flora looked over her shoulder at him. 'Is she mad, do you mean?'

Carl coloured up. 'No, that wasn't what I meant at all.'

'She's every bit as sane as you are, if that's anything to judge by. Don't be forgetting the sandwiches you asked for.'

The male eagle had been off in search of food since first light. The fast, forced on them by the thick fog, had left the whole family hungry. His beady eye searched for the merest morsel which might satisfy even a corner. He quartered the island, swooping back and forth with his catches. There was no shortage of prey. Hundreds of animals of varying sizes, kept from feeding by the bad weather, were out scavenging on this fine day.

The female, still wary, though the memory of the plundering of their nest was beginning to fade, stood guard while arching her wings wide, as if she was about to glide off the ledge, using the sun and wind to dry herself out thoroughly.

She watched critically as the two eaglets practised their

pounces, getting ready for the day when they would try their wings properly. Gripping the twigs on the edge of the nest, they too spread their wings, then launched themselves into the air only to tumble across each other and squabble on the floor of the nest. Quickly they recovered their dignity and clambered back up to try again. Although they seemed to be playing, and they could not know how important this would be for their future, instinct told them that it was part of their struggle for survival. As their hunger grew daily with their size the need to satisfy it for themselves increased, using their own hunting instincts, rather than waiting for their parents.

It would only be days now before they began to try the real thing.

As Shona left the croft the rest of the family was hard at work. Her mother was pegging out freshly laundered snowy sheets to toss themselves dry in the clean, bright air. Her father and two brothers were bending their backs as they turned the damp hay over and over. The wind picked up some of the drier grass strands which caught momentarily on the barbed wire fencing before rushing off with it out to sea. Everyone, except for Shona was busy, and happy to be released from their imprisonment.

What she wanted to do was go straight up to the Big House and call for Carl, like her brothers called for their friends. But she could not help smiling as she tried to imagine herself marching up to the grand front door of the Laird's house and banging on the big, brass knocker.

Going anywhere near the Big House was out of the question. So what should she do? She could go down to the beach but after the experience with the quicksand she could not imagine Carl going back there again for awhile.

For that matter whilst she was anxious to see Carl again, there was no reason why he should feel the same way. After all he had a sister and family of his own. He did not need her company.

He had stayed with her yesterday, but maybe that was

107

only out of politeness, or simply because he could not get rid of her!

Today, if he saw her coming, he might well hide or run away. She had known people do that before now. Soon after she first went to school Shona had followed Fiona MacBratney, the garage mechanic's daughter, everywhere. Fiona had long blonde hair which she sometimes wore in a pigtail which she could almost sit on. Shona had never seen her until the day they met at school. Fiona lived right down at the south end of the island and from the moment Shona first set eyes on her she followed Fiona everywhere, convinced that she was some kind of fairy or special being.

Fiona quite clearly had never seen anybody like Shona either but for quite different reasons. She did not understand about Shona's inability to talk properly and thought the way she walked was very odd indeed. Fiona's reaction to this was to run away whenever Shona came into sight as if Shona were a demon. Shona made things worse with her frantic attempts to follow Fiona, calling after her in a language which Fiona had never heard before. Poor Fiona spent many a break-time during her first days at school locked in the lavatory, hiding from Shona.

Shona feared Carl might easily react in exactly the same way, and who could blame him?

Oh, well, she sighed to herself, there was only one way to find out and that was to try. But where to look? If neither the beach or the Big House were possible that left only one other place that she could think of – but on his own would he be able to find his way back there?

'Everywhere still feels so damp,' Beverly complained, helping herself to more coffee.

'But at least the fog has cleared now,' Howard pointed out, 'and you can get out for some fresh air.'

Donna ostentatiously mopped her streaming eyes with a pink tissue. 'I'm going back to bed.'

'You haven't got a bed,' Beverly said quietly.

'I just want to lie down, on anything.'

Howard looked at them both and sighed. 'You two aren't getting much out of this experience, are you?'

'Except post nasal drip,' Donna muttered to herself – she no longer expected sympathy.

'I'd hoped it would be so much fun for us all. An opportunity to try a different way of life in a different environment.'

'I liked my old environment well enough,' Donna growled.

'The trouble with you, young lady, is you've had everything too easy for too long. It's time you got up off your butt and did something. When I was your age . . .'

Donna groaned.

'Don't give me attitude!' Howard barked. 'That's your problem. You not only want to be the fairy on top of the tree you want all the presents from under as well. Well, let me tell you real life is not like that. There's more to living than planning your next raid on Bloomingdales and Europe isn't all about Harrods and Galeries Lafayette.'

Beverly put a hand on Howard's arm. 'Take it easy.'

Howard snatched his arm away. 'She's the one who takes it easy all the time. Look at Carl, he's making the best of things here, trying new things . . .'

'Bird-watching!'

'Whatever. He's exploring and he isn't just moping round the house wondering where his next set of bedroom furniture is coming from.'

There was a knock at the door at which Howard pulled up short. Flora put her head round. 'Mr MacPherson would like a word, if you've a moment. The ferry came in late last night with the building materials you've been expecting.'

'Great! Now we can get moving again.' Howard got up to leave and then turned back for one last word with Donna. 'You think over what I've been saying. See you later, Bev.'

Flora was about to follow Howard out when she remembered something else. 'Miss Donna, there's some enormous great parcels in the courtyard for you too.'

The cloud evaporated from Donna's face. She threw her

tissue down and ran from the room shouting, 'Fantastic! My new bedroom furniture's arrived.'

'Flora, do you know where Carl is?' Beverly asked.

'He was away early this morning, Mrs Kleinberger. He said something about going to see a diver.'

'A diver? I hope he isn't thinking of swimming, I'm sure it's far too cold for that.'

'I think a diver's some sort of a bird.'

'Oh,' said Beverly looking mystified.

'Can I clear away in here now? I've lit a nice fire in the sitting room. I've put the post and the day before yesterday's newspapers in there, they came over with the ferry.'

'Thanks, Flora, there'll be a lot to catch up with.'

'Aye, no rest for the wicked, is there?'


Shona had left the road and was picking her way round the end of a marshy lochan when she thought she heard singing. She glanced up and saw Red Angus swaying across the heather towards her.

He had come over with the late ferry but the delay to his return journey had simply given him even more opportunity to enjoy his favourite pastime, drinking whisky.

'Hey, you there!' Red shouted, waving his bottle in the air.

Shona pretended not to hear and kept on walking.

'I see you! Don't think I don't. And I know who you are.'

She tried to change direction but the ground was too marshy. There was no choice but to continue on her present route and try to pass him, or to turn back.

'Shona MacLeod,' he droned on, 'you come here to me.'

Shona had no intention of doing any such thing; she did not trust either of the Angus brothers sober, let alone drunk. If she could she would have run but she knew she could not run fast enough to escape. He was only metres away and staggering closer every second. Her only hope was to dodge round him at the last minute.

'Do you wanna hear a secret?' Red whispered.

Shona shook her head. There were just two more steps

before she had to take her opportunity of escape and she was watching for her chance, hoping that when the moment came her body would respond.

'I've got money,' he gasped, pulling a thick wad of notes from his pocket. 'Have you ever seen as much money as that?'

Red Angus was so close now that gales of his whisky-sodden breath enveloped her.

As they drew level Shona dodged off the path to the left. At the same moment, drunk but not slow, he shot out an arm to make a grab at her but in avoiding his grubby hand Shona lost her balance so they both went sprawling.

Panic-stricken she tried to crawl away from him but he grabbed her firmly by the arm, thrusting his face up close.

'Try to run off, would you? You think you're really somebody, you MacLeods, don't you?'

Shona could not answer, she tried to shake her head but succeeded only in trembling with fear.

'You're a stuck-up lot, so you are. Well, I'm as good as you any day. Look at this!' He looked down at his empty hand and realised that in grabbing Shona he had dropped his money which the wind was spreading across the heather, peeling it off the wad, note by note, as if it were being counted by invisible fingers.

When Red tried to capture the disappearing notes Shona saw her chance and edged away as quickly as she could.

'You come and help!' he shouted after her but Shona kept on going.

The last she saw of him he was crawling about on his hands and knees in the mud trying to gather up his money.

'I'll not forget this, Shona MacLeod,' Red Angus shouted after her. 'I'll get even with you for this. You and your whole family.'

Carl had been watching the divers from behind the grass mound for what seemed like hours. He was thinking of starting the sandwiches which Flora had cut when he spotted Shona stumbling towards him.

During the rest of the journey to the loch she had had time to recover her composure a little but Red Angus's threat still rang in her ears. She waved awkwardly.

Although he waved back Carl was not sure how pleased he was to see her. Carl enjoyed his own company.

But without her he would never have found the divers he had spent the morning watching with such great pleasure as they dived in the loch for food, watched and imitated by their sooty chicks.

Come to that, but for Shona he might not have been watching *anything* today, he would probably have been dead!

'Hi, Shona,' he whispered as she drew near. 'I'm sorry I got your name wrong yesterday, by the way. Flora put me straight.'

Much as she was grateful that Carl had got her name right she was not very happy that he had been talking to Flora about her. The whole island would probably know about their meeting by the end of the day.

'Black-throated divers they're called,' Carl said, jerking a thumb over his shoulder towards the birds.

Shona nodded. Like Flora she tended to accept the birds without necessarily knowing all their names. It was something that often led to misunderstandings between islanders and tourists. The tourists, having sometimes travelled hundreds, if not thousands, of miles to see some rare species, were apt to get very annoyed when the locals told them they could not tell them exactly where to find a particular bird.

'Would you like a sandwich?' Carl held them out to Shona.

Shona shyly took one. It seemed a good sign to her. If he was willing to share his food then perhaps he was willing to accept her company. Those were the rules of island hospitality.

# Twelve

For the next two weeks there were, to the islanders' astonishment, no major changes wrought on the island.

Not that that prevented all the rumours from spreading, being polished up and improved upon as well as new ones being created. Anyone who scorned even the most outrageous suggestions earned only pitying looks from those around who were older and wiser.

The young eagles, watched by their fond parents, had begun their first attempts at flying. After hours of tentatively climbing up on to the edge of the nest, then going back down, eventually the stronger of the two, urged on by demonstrations by the male and encouraging noises from the throat of the female, had launched itself into its first, faltering glide. Its relatively feeble wings spread wide, it seemed to have no idea of how to control its direction. Losing height all the way, it looked destined to crash into the exposed rocks on one side or the other of the valley before eventually it managed to land, more by accident than design, on a rock thirty metres below the nest.

There it stood, breathing hard, sufficiently unnerved by its rapid descent to be happy to stay there for ever rather than try again.

The weaker of the two, having seen what had happened to its companion, was even more reluctant to leave the safety of the nest. Only an impressive aerial display put on by both its parents and a distinct fear, as the last in the nest, that it was about to be deserted, persuaded it to try.

Its first attempt was almost its last. Lacking the strength to arch its wings sufficiently, it fell like a dead leaf from the edge of the nest. Only a reflex reaction of self-preservation and accidentally finding a thermal, which kept it airborne, prevented disaster.

Yet it gave the other eaglet encouragement to have another try. Soon they both made reasonably successful flights, if rather clumsy landings, but it was still possible to tell which of the two was the stronger. It would be another three weeks before their flying would be judged strong enough, or competent enough, to begin learning the first principles of hunting for food. But at least the female had regained her freedom.

Mr MacLeod, with the help of his wife and sons, whom he refused to let out of his sight for fear they would end up in worse trouble, dried out the hay they had cut and gathered it up into a neat, round stack at the back of the house, to be used for the animals' winter feed. When the stack had cooled, or at the first sign of a strong wind, a tarpaulin would be slung over it, held down by lumps of rock hanging from lengths of rope. Until then similarly weighted old fishing nets were used which, in Shona's mind, made the stacks look as if they wore hairnets.

Both Sandy and Andrew were tired of not being allowed off the croft. 'It is the holiday, after all!' Sandy protested.

'You've your brother to blame for that. If I cannot trust you to stay out of trouble then I'd rather you were where I can keep an eye on you. It's not as if we're short of work to do, anyway. We'll be getting the sheep in for shearing soon and there's the peats to be cut for winter yet.'

The boys groaned in unison. Usually peat cutting was a pleasant interlude, an excuse for a picnic on the moor with a little hard work and carrying back, in the endless weeks of freedom and pleasure which they normally enjoyed. This year it was just one more task on a seemingly never ending list.

Nor were the brothers any happier that Shona, who had no work to do, was still allowed to roam freely.

'It isn't fair. Why shouldn't she have to work like us?' demanded Andrew.

Mr MacLeod shook his head. 'And what could she do?'

'Well, you let her wander off. You won't let us off the croft even when we've finished work for the day.'

'It's you two I cannot trust. It's no good complaining. The time to think about that was before you got yourselves into trouble, not now.'

It was on the tip of Andrew's tongue to protest that he was only in trouble because of Shona. He only hit the boy because he had been rude about her. But Andrew knew that it would be unfair to blame her, besides blaming Shona for anything usually made things worse not better.

Work was the order of the day up at the Big House too. The conversion of the old coach house into a modern communications centre was almost complete. The technicians were installing the last of the modern equipment and the building work was long since finished.

That should have been good news for Donna who had been impatiently waiting for Donald to be allowed to come and erect her bedroom furniture. Unfortunately Beverly wanted him to do some rebuilding of the kitchen first and as this work did not meet with Flora's approval, she delayed it at every turn.

'What about my bedroom?' Donna wailed. The day the furniture had arrived she had excitedly ripped the cardboard wrappings off the flat-packed units and strewn the contents around her room where they had lain ever since.

'Why not take a journey into the unknown?' her father suggested.

Donna looked puzzled. 'How do you mean?'

Howard went and borrowed a hammer and a screwdriver from Donald which he handed over to Donna. 'It says in all the adverts that this stuff can be erected by a twelve-year-old kid. If you are so anxious to get the job done, why not do it yourself? I kind of like to think that you're every bit as clever as any twelve-year-old.'

'Daddy!'

Howard shrugged. 'Well, it's either that or wait!'

To her father's amazement, Donna changed into her designer jeans and set to work. It was not easy. Unfortunately in the excitement of unwrapping she had not only muddled up some of the sections, so that the wardrobe unit appeared to have five doors instead of four, she had also lost one of the plans which had somehow managed to get burnt with the wrappings. This meant constructing an overhead unit from whatever happened to be left over, with nothing to guide her. It took six bad-tempered attempts but she made it finally and although some of the units were a little wobbly until Howard, impressed by what she had achieved, went round tightening up some of the screws, it looked pretty good in the end. All Donald had to do was fasten the assembled units to the wall, which Beverly released him to do during a couple of hours one morning, and the job was finished.

When Howard and Beverly went up to admire the result they were quick to praise her.

'There, honey, it looks great,' Howard said, putting his arm round his daughter's shoulder, 'and you must have got a great feeling of achievement doing it.'

Donna grinned back at him. 'What I got was blisters!'

'But you have to admit it's good doing things yourself.'

'I didn't have much choice, even Carl refused to help.'

Howard looked puzzled. 'Where is Carl? He goes out before any of us are up and I don't see him all day. What *is* he up to?'

Beverly shrugged. 'Bird-watching – what else?'

In fact he and Shona, who had spent most of every day together, had done much more than bird-watching. With Shona to show him round they had explored a great deal of the island. She had been able to show him all the things Uncle James had shown her. Carl was constantly amazed and with her help he had seen otters at play, seals basking with their young pups. They had visited an ancient, stone burial mound and a circle of stone monoliths, not even shown in the island guide book.

Carl always carried that and the bird book with him because Shona never spoke or tried to explain the things she took him to see. Carl thought it weird that he was willing to follow her, not knowing where they were going, or what they were going to see. Occasionally he could follow their route in the guide book but sometimes he was totally lost.

When they arrived Shona would silently point until Carl saw what he was supposed to see but it was quite a guessing game. He did not know the size of the object, whether it was still or moving, animal, vegetable or mineral, close up or far away.

'Do you mean those rocks?' Carl would ask. Shona shook her head. 'The sea? I can't see anything but sea!' Shona would point harder, a little higher up. Sometimes she would lift his binoculars towards his eyes and perhaps then he would at last see the latest wonder.

One day it was a flock of large, yellow-headed birds, which looked, through the glasses, as if they had been designed by Walt Disney. Carl discovered they were gannets and they spent a morning totally fascinated by their *kamikaze* diving into the sea.

The gannets would casually fly just above and parallel with the water until they spotted a fish, then they would suddenly plummet, head first after it in a dive that looked as if it would lead to their certain destruction, only to emerge, triumphant, moments later and repeat the whole per-formance.

Shona loved looking through Carl's binoculars. It was something she had never tried before and in many ways it reminded her of her beloved, lost piece of flawed glass, though now the images were quite different.

'Here, let me focus them for you,' Carl would say before handing them over.

Shona did not mind whether they were focused or not.

Although she enjoyed the crystal clear, close-up images of birds and animals she had only previously seen from a distance, she equally liked looking at the fuzzy kaleidoscopes of colour she got when the glasses were not focused properly. There was something about the colours and textures she saw that way which really appealed to her, reminding her of the colours of the tweed cloth she had seen in the weaving sheds.

Although at first Shona's silence bothered Carl he grew accustomed to it and when he realised, by the expressions on her face, that she was perfectly content as she was, he began to relax. He even talked less himself. Sometimes hours would pass in which they did not exchange a single word.

Shona had not been so happy since her Uncle James had left. For the first time in her life, she was not the one being shown something, she was the one doing the showing. She had somebody who was happy to learn from her. It gave her a growing feeling of confidence in herself. Until now she had always had the feeling that she relied completely on other people, to the extent that she was a permanent millstone around their necks. She never felt that when she was with Carl.

So it was not only a shock but an enormous disappointment when one day Carl did not turn up at their pre-arranged meeting place, just off the main road close to the Big House.

A hollow loneliness, which in the past she would have accepted as normal but recently had grown unused to, settled over her as she waited and waited. Still Carl did not arrive.

'It all works!' Carl could not hide the disbelief in his voice. Surrounded by the very latest electronic equipment in the coach house, he was behaving like a kid in a toyshop.

'Pretty amazing, I agree,' admitted Howard. 'I have to say that from time to time I thought the whole project was doomed to failure but not now.' He looked round with deep satisfaction at the array of monitors, printers and key-boards which filled most of the available space apart from his own glass-walled office which he had had built into one corner.

The fax machine bleeped and they both rushed over to watch as material from Howard's New York office, thousands of miles away, was printed out before their eyes.

'Makes you almost homesick, doesn't it?' said Howard quietly.

'It's a good job you can't transport people this way,' said Carl, 'or Donna would be the first candidate!'

'What about you, Carl?'

'Me? I'm happy just the way I am.'

'You adapt more easily than your mother or Donna. They're more home types, if you know what I mean. Old stock of America. You and me belong on the list of New Americans. Refugees and wanderers, pioneers who are always restless, wanting to explore new ground.'

But Carl was not listening. 'Dad, can I try out the computer graphics. I did some at school but there was always too much else to do to really spend time on it and I've got a few ideas I'd like to work through.'

'Tell you the truth, I'd be glad if you'd hang around for a while. I like the things these machines do but I can't pretend I understand them like you do. Until I get a couple of people up from London to operate for me I'd be grateful for some help now the installation guys have left.'

Carl was in seventh heaven. Lost in the delights of creation he disappeared into a world of his own from which he did not emerge until lunchtime, when Flora came out to remind him to go and eat. It was only then that he remembered Shona and felt a surge of guilt. But then, he told himself, it was not as if they had a definite arrangement, she would understand he could not turn up every single day. He would go and see her again in a couple of days. He felt very torn but the novelty and excitement of the new computer set-up won hands down and time passed very quickly in front of the screen.

Day after day Shona trudged up the road to their meeting place but there was no sign of Carl. She sat on a large rock, where she could see who passed up and down the road, patiently waiting for him. She tried to convince herself that he would turn up, that he wanted to see her, but in her heart, as time crept on, she had an awful feeling that Carl, bored with her company, would never come again.

But every day she managed to convince herself that he would be waiting for her and she set out again. She would stay long after she grew hungry before she headed for home.

One day on the way home she was overtaken by her schoolteacher, Miss Ferguson, who pulled up to give her a lift. Although it was a long walk Shona did not really want a lift which would get her back home in minutes. Time was not something that she was short of, since Carl had deserted her. The long walk home helped to pass time but it would have been difficult and embarrassing to try to refuse, so Shona reluctantly caught up with the car.

Miss Ferguson leant across to open the door for Shona. 'Hop in, Shona,' she said and instantly regretted the phrase. 'Have you been enjoying the holidays?'

In spite of her true feelings Shona managed a sort of nod.

'I've just come back from Venice.' She told Shona all about the wonderful art treasures and beautiful buildings she had visited.

Every year Miss Ferguson saved up so that she could spend at least three weeks somewhere warm and foreign which she would spend the first few weeks of term telling her pupils about, showing them slides and souvenirs she had brought back.

The islanders were sharply divided into those who did or did not take holidays. Those who did were viewed by the rest with a mixture of envy and scorn. Fergus the Post said, 'All that hot weather drains the strength out of them.'

It was perfectly true they had difficulty getting acclimatised on their return. Miss Ferguson, who was wearing a grey silk dress to show off her tan, had goose pimples on her exposed arms.

To Shona, who had never in her life been off the island, foreign places started at the end of the island's quay. She viewed them all, whether it was the mainland where the boys went to school, America, which had swallowed up Uncle James, or Venice, with deep suspicion. At school Miss Ferguson had told them about people, years ago, who believed that the earth was flat and that if you went too far, you fell off, over the edges.

Though Shona did not believe that, she had an idea of a kind of limbo, where people floated endlessly until they could return to the island. She told herself this could not be true, but as she found it impossible to visualise the people she knew having an existence in another place which she could not see and as they almost never appeared in the photographs they brought back with them (and never on the postcards they sent), Shona dismissed the idea that it was possible to live anywhere else. The nearest Shona could get to her version of the truth was that people were sent to what she regarded as foreign places as some kind of punishment. The only person who did not fit wholly into that idea was Uncle James.

'It's Fair day tomorrow, isn't it?' Miss Ferguson said as she dropped Shona off where the main road passed the end of Shona's track. 'I expect I'll see you all there. Goodbye!'

Shona watched Miss Ferguson's neat, white mini until it disappeared round a bend in the road before she turned for home. Perhaps her father had forgotten all about the Fair, the annual animal sale, to which they had threatened to send Morag.

Indeed when she got home her family were busy shearing the sheep which they had brought back from the mountain slope.

The noise and clamour around the house was frightful as the apprehensive, protesting sheep were each turned over on their backs and their fleeces removed with huge shears. Lambs separated from their mother ewes bleated piteously, as the two were rarely in the same compound but Shona laughed as she watched the freshly sheared sheep, suddenly looking so skinny, go leaping off into the air the moment they were released. The young sheep, with their tiny, polished hooves looked more like toys than real animals once their ragged fleeces had been removed.

Like most occasions on the island, sheering was treated not just as work but also as a social occasion. Other families from neighbouring crofts had come to help not only with the round up but with the shearing itself. The MacLeod family would do the same for them in return.

At meal times there was always plenty of gossip as they all sat round on the pile of tightly rolled, springy fleeces to eat and drink the food Mrs MacLeod provided.

But this year the gathering was more solemn than usual.

'We may not have this job to trouble us next year,' Mr MacLeod kept saying with a sigh and they would all nod, looking down at their food for they all realised the seriousness of his position. 'I was wondering if I should save myself the trouble and take the whole lot down to tomorrow's Fair. It'll be no good trying to sell them after that.'

'But if you do that you'll likely get the lease renewed and you'll have sold off a fine flock which you won't be able to replace for a twelve month.'

'Aye, and if I don't, I'll have a flock with no feed for them.'

'You know fine we'd all help out.'

Mr MacLeod nodded glumly.

'You might be better off without that land anyway.'

'How do you make that out?'

'Aren't those damned eagles for ever taking the lambs? Somebody should shoot the blessed things.'

Mr MacLeod shook his head. 'I won't have that.'

'Because it is against the law?'

'I wouldn't shoot them even if the law said I could. I think they are wonderful creatures and they have been on this earth a great deal longer than we have. I'll not begrudge them the odd lamb.'

122

'Rather them than the Laird, eh?'

Shona wished that she could have talked to Carl about her father's problem. Maybe he would be able to persuade his father to let them stay. But the chances of even seeing Carl, let alone being capable of discussing anything, seemed very remote.

What was clear to Shona was that far from her father forgetting the Fair, it was very much on his mind. Whether the threat to sell Morag had been remembered she did not know but suddenly she was overwhelmed by a feeling that everything was coming to an end at once. Not only had she lost her new-found friend but now, as well as the prospect of having to join her brothers at the mainland school, suddenly it seemed the whole MacLeod family might all be leaving the island.

This fitted in entirely with Shona's view of punishment. They were to live the rest of their lives in exile like the people in the stories Uncle James had told.

The prospect of floating in limbo, trying to atone for the wrongs they had committed, filled Shona with horror but her more immediate dread centred on her beloved Morag.

At dusk the weaker eaglet was stranded on a rock ledge close to the nest. It had made several attempts to get back but each time had failed to land properly and now it was too late and too dark, to try. Both the parents had flown round it in urgent circles to encourage it to try once more but by now the creature was too cold and weak from hunger.

It crouched, its feathers fluffed out as it attempted to keep out the worst of the cold. Alone, for the first time in its life, its parents doubted it would survive the night.

# Thirteen

As the first pink tinges of dawn washed over the clouds of mist which hung above the lochans, the smaller eaglet was still hunched on the outcrop of rock. Even under the protection of the fluffed-out feathers it felt cold and stiff. Having burned up so much energy the previous day in flight and throughout the night in self-preservation, it had used up all its reserves. It must eat soon or it would die. The parents knew this too and were already looking for food.

For the time of day there was even more activity than usual on the island. Men, women and children were not only up but out, rounding up animals, scrubbing them down, getting the muck out of tails.

The eagles, though puzzled, regarded it as only a minor irritation, their concentration was solely on food. The stronger of the two eaglets flew with the parents and, whilst not hunting itself, eagerly watched the male.

Down at the foot of the Black Mountain the male had spotted a small flock of mallards. The drakes were making a great commotion, fighting amongst themselves whilst the ducks, pretending not to notice, swirled round the loch ducking their heads excitedly beneath the water, watching out for the winners. The eagle circled above them unnoticed, biding his time.

At the height of the scrap the losing drake beat the water with his wings and webbed feet. The others, realising he was about to escape, did the same, churning the surface of the water into a white froth as they took off with loud, threatening quacks.

Silently, keeping the sun ahead of him so that he threw no warning shadows, the eagle gradually lost height at the same time accelerating to keep pace with the noisy, flapping ducks.

The escaping drake was too concerned about the pursuit of the other drakes to be aware of the much more real danger which threatened him from above. They were gaining on him so he wheeled off suddenly to the right.

This was the moment the eagle had been waiting for. He swooped down fast. The drakes, who had been occupied solely in giving chase, saw the eagle. Their calls changed to ones of clamour and alarm but too late.

The eagle extended its talons in mid-flight and, bending its legs slightly to act as shock absorbers, stabbed them savagely into the drake's back, closed them to rip the internal organs, then swiftly adjusted the power of his flight to allow for the extra weight he was now carrying.

The glossy head of the hapless drake dropped as it died instantly.

Other, braver birds might have mobbed the eagle, chattered round his head to drive him away, but the drakes had lost all heart for a fight with the smell of death on the morning air. Realising there was nothing they could do, they flew off to safety while the eagle carried his prey back to the eyrie, transferring it nimbly from claws to beak the instant before he landed.

Having ripped apart the dead bird he flew out above the ledge where the eaglet was stranded and dropped a portion of the meat. Soon the weakened eaglet was reviving itself on morsels of flesh hacked from the carcass of the drake.

Shona had slept badly. The moment she woke she remembered that it was Fair Day which usually filled her with excitement, but not this year. Fair Day was one of the largest social gatherings on the island. Although yesterday Morag had not been discussed, everyone had been too busy with the shearing, Shona was certain of the answer. Their house-cow, friend and companion of her whole childhood, was about to be sold off.

Her worst fears were confirmed at breakfast.

'This is the last milk we'll be having from her,' her mother said bluntly, as she tipped the creamy milk over the porridge. Mrs MacLeod caught Shona's expression. 'It's no good pulling a face, young Shona. The animals are here to keep us, not the other way round, and if they outlive their usefulness they have to go, that's all there is to it.' She shook her head. 'It's always a mistake to give animals names, it turns them into pets. Now eat up or you'll be left behind.'

Shona's appetite went. The only minor consolation was that with having to drive Morag down to the Fair the family would be walking slowly enough for Shona to keep pace with them.

'Are the sheep going too?' asked Andrew.

'Only a few old ewes past their prime. You and your father can look after them. Shona and I will take Morag . . .' she shook her head at her tactlessness and quickly corrected herself, '. . . the cow!'

Andrew grinned. 'I don't know what all the fuss is about. It's only an old cow.'

But Sandy did not share his feelings. 'I'll miss her. She's a grand old cow. Better-tempered than most, too. She doesn't kick the bucket over and lash out at you when you try to get near her, like some.'

'Hush now, and get on with your breakfasts. We've a deal to do before we go.'

Shona bent over her porridge to hide the tear that was sliding down her face. It dropped with a watery plop to mix with the creamy goodness of Morag's milk.

'Why are you cooking breakfast, Mom?' Carl asked.

'Because Donna refused to run the risk of chipping her nail varnish.'

Carl laughed. 'That wasn't what I meant. What's happened to Flora – why isn't she doing it?'

'She wanted the day off for the Fair. She and Donald have to bring some animals to it and they wanted to make an early start. Go get the others, everything's ready.'

Carl called upstairs to his sister and then went to collect his father who had gone over to the coach house early to do some work on his speech.

Carl found him frantically crossing out words on a scrappy sheet of paper.

'How's it going?'

'Badly! Why they need me to speak at this thing beats the hell out of me!'

'Why do it then?'

'Because MacPherson says everyone *expects* it. How they can "expect" it when there hasn't been a Laird on the island in years I don't know.' He handed Carl the sheet of paper. 'What do you think?'

Carl tried to read it but the piece of paper was too covered with corrections which smothered the spidery writing of the original text. 'I think that when it comes to the time you won't be able to read a word of this!'

Howard sighed. 'I guess you're right at that!'

'How about if, after breakfast, you dictate it to me and I punch it up on the word processor?'

Howard's face lit up. 'Great idea! All this creative work makes me hungry – let's go eat.'

Beverly, having altered the kitchen to her own taste, with only a few compromises to Flora's, had enjoyed the chance to cook breakfast and even Donna was delighted with the results.

'Corn muffins! Gee, Mom!' She gave her mother a big hug.

'You're welcome!'

'And hash-browns and waffles,' Carl shouted.

'Is that a *real* jar of maple syrup – or a mirage?' Howard asked. 'What did you do, smuggle it into the country?'

'No,' Beverly said with a proud smile, 'I rang the storekeeper . . .'

'Mr MacKay?'

'. . .and said that if he didn't get me some you'd close up the store.'

'Bev! What an awful thing to say!'

'If you don't want some, just say the word! There is some cold porridge left over from yesterday. I could heat it up for you, if you'd rather.'

'This looks wonderful. And the eggs are done easy over, just the way I like them!'

They all sat down, ate far too much and ended up suffering from heartburn and homesickness.

'Boy, this takes me back!' Donna said wistfully, as she mopped the corners of her mouth with her napkin.

'I may have to *go* back one day soon,' said Howard quietly.

'Can't we all go?' pleaded Donna.

Beverly's brow creased. 'Why's that, honey?'

'Some things in New York and Chicago.'

'I thought you'd just spent a fortune on this communications network to sort out problems like that.'

'Problems on paper you can sort out that way easily enough, but sometimes the only way to sort people out is eyeball to eyeball. There are, right now, one or two people who need a head-to-head to get them back on the straight and narrow. I could maybe drop in and see how my mother is while I'm in Chicago. I hope it won't be necessary to go at all. I'd like to have this place up-and-running before we go back. Glenn sent some interesting papers up overnight.'

Donna had not forgotten the name Glenn. He was the whizz-kid accountant she blamed totally for their being stuck out on this rock! 'Has he had another bright idea?'

The sarcasm was lost on Howard. 'Word is there may be some tax changes coming up in the UK Autumn Budget that could affect our position over the island.'

Donna bounced up and down on her chair. 'Are we going to have to sell it? Oh, don't I wish!'

Howard smiled in spite of himself. 'The changes aren't that drastic, honey, but they may seriously affect the level of investment we can make here. Enough! Time to set out for the Fair. Best bib and tucker, don't forget!'

Beverly pulled a face. 'I'm so concerned with keeping warm I'm not sure I have anything I can wear.'

Howard put his arm round Beverly. 'Bev, I just know you'll knock their eyes out!'

Fair Day was such a mixture of work and pleasure that the islanders neither wore their Sunday go-to-church clothes nor their working ones but usually a mixture of both. It was not possible to drive animals, who constantly strayed from the road, without boots and the likelihood of rain before the day was over made some kind of protection vital. But within those limits the islanders dressed up for the event.

Shona had on an old oilskin and wellington boots but the coat was open and beneath it she wore her green tweed skirt with a jersey that was so yellow it was almost gold. She had on her head a green tammy her mother had knitted, which set off the colour of her hair and eyes.

Morag seemed aware of her fate. She trudged down the road at the slowest of paces taking every opportunity to sample the juicy grass along the verges as she wandered back and forth across the road, like a yacht tacking into the wind. Like most animals on the island she had no respect for vehicles and her road-sense was based on a simple faith that anything that came would stop if she was in the way.

To Shona's enormous embarrassment when the Laird's Range Rover came it too had to pull up while Morag shambled across in front of it. Shona was relieved that her mother was too busy looking after Morag, trying to persuade her out of the way with slaps on her vast rump, to notice Carl waving to Shona from the front seat next to his father.

Shona pretended not to have seen him. After all, he had been avoiding her for days but she could not help noticing the curious expressions on the faces of his family when the car was finally able to pull away.

*

'Who on earth was that?' Donna immediately asked.

Howard answered for Carl. 'Shona MacLeod.'

'Isn't that the sister of those boys who beat Carl up?' Beverly asked as she peered out through the back window.

Carl tried to slump down in his seat in the hope that he might turn invisible.

'I think that exaggerates the position a little, Bev,' Howard said, 'but she is from that family.'

'What a weird kid!' said Donna with distaste. 'Why can't she walk properly? I think she looks real spooky.'

'She's OK.' Carl interrupted hotly. 'Just because she isn't a Madonna Wanna-be!'

'How come you know her?' Howard asked quietly, slowing down to negotiate a man with some calves that leapt and kicked all over the road.

Carl was not going to admit to the quicksands. 'I met her a few times while I was out bird-watching.'

'Now we know what kind of birds you were really watching!' said Donna. 'I can't say I admire your taste in women, Carl.'

'I hardly know the kid,' Carl said tersely and then felt ashamed that he was denying not only the companionship he had shared with Shona but, more importantly, the fact that he probably owed her his life.

'Just keep her away from me, that's all I ask!' Donna said. 'The sight of her gives me the willies!'

Even though Beverly understood and, to a certain extent shared, Donna's fixation with perfection she could not let the remark pass. 'I think that's a little unkind, Donna. She can't help the way she is, poor little girl.'

The dislike on the part of his sister and the rather patronising tone his mother used made Carl think about Shona. For somebody who had so much trouble walking they had certainly covered some miles together, whereas neither Donna or his mother had even ventured out of the Big House, except, like now, in the Range Rover. Also, Shona's knowledge of the island and the birds and animals who made it their home was incredible. That, and the way she had thought of rescuing him from his own foolishness and ignorance, proved beyond doubt that there was nothing wrong with her mind.

The fact that she looked a little odd, had trouble controlling her movements and could almost not talk at all (not that they even knew) seemed to him poor reasons to judge somebody and find them wanting.

The trouble was that, to his shame, having denied nearly all knowledge of Shona, he could hardly correct them now. He stared moodily out at the passing landscape for the remainder of the journey.

# Fourteen

Almost everyone on the island, except for Dr MacGregor and Mrs MacLeish, who had at last gone into labour in the cottage hospital, had gathered for Fair Day. Many travelling people turned up every year. Some sold things, others played musical instruments and collected pennies and some collected more than pennies by gambling with the islanders.

To the islanders, the most important part of the day was the sale of their surplus animals but the social side was never far away and it was a noisy, colourful scene with celebrations that would continue long into the night.

For over two hundred years it had always been held on a strip of land at the south end of the island alongside an old inn. The inn, which had special licence to sell drinks all day, did a roaring trade. Beside the inn there was a rotting, wooden pier which had half collapsed into the sea. The site had been chosen originally when this was the island's only quay, where the boats moored to carry off the animals that were chiefly bought by people from the mainland.

Now the pier was derelict, replaced by the stone quay at the north end, so the boats could no longer come to collect the animals. Consequently there were those who said the Fair ought to be moved but most of the islanders disagreed. They liked to cling to the old ways, even if that meant driving those animals destined for the mainland right across the island. There were associations with good luck on this site that many islanders believed would be changed for the worse by moving the Fair elsewhere.

By the time Shona, her mother and Morag eventually arrived the Laird, much to his relief, had made his opening speech and the auction was well under way. The colourful clothing of the Laird's family, only equalled by the sprinkling of tourists, made it easy to pick them out amongst the large crowd. But Shona had resolved to keep well away from the Laird's family. It was not only that she had not forgiven Carl for deserting her but she did not want to be seen talking to him by the whole island!

Her father and mother were kept busy with the auction, Mrs MacLeod especially. Morag, normally a quiet, placid beast, did not like the noisy bustle of the crowd. She decided to try to leave soon after she arrived and was numbered lot 302 by a white, oval label with large, black numbers which was stuck on her rump. It took all of Mrs MacLeod's strength and powers of persuasion to keep Morag there at all.

Sandy and Andrew, able to escape their father's eye at long last, rapidly disappeared into the crowd with their friends. There was no shortage of mischief for them to get into on Fair Day. The secure doors of crates, used for bringing hens or ducks to the auction, had been known to open themselves mysteriously. Men who sat too long watching the auction often discovered that their shoelaces had managed to become seriously entangled.

Shona, always more of a watcher than a doer, enjoyed the fun of the pranks they played but the part she liked most of all was going round the fringe of the auction where the travelling people set out their wares. There were no proper stalls, the goods were laid out on the ground in the suitcases and bags in which the people brought them.

As well as the practical articles offered for sale, sheets, towels, anoraks and dresses, there was also bright, shiny jewellery and all kinds of beautifully coloured soaps and perfumes that gave off wonderful smells.

Shona loved rummaging around amongst the stalls trying to decide how to spend the money she had saved all year. There was no hurry, she had all day, and looking around trying to decide was the best part. In the past she had wandered round them with Uncle James but today she had to do it alone.

There was one 'stall' Shona liked above all others. It was run by a little, pudding-bag of a woman called Old Annie.

Old Annie dressed from head to foot in black. Her face was nut-brown covered with hundreds of fine lines, so deep they reminded Shona of a ploughed field. Although she rarely smoked it she was never seen without a small, charred, clay pipe which she kept clamped between the gaps in her yellow teeth and, over one eye, she wore a black patch.

Uncle James had told Shona that he thought Old Annie was a pirate who had been shipwrecked and who was selling all her ill-gotten gains to raise the money to buy another ship in which to sail round the world again robbing more people.

Old Annie had been coming, her pack on her bent back, as long as anybody could remember and she always laid out her wares alongside the inn wall, facing the sun and where there was more shelter from any wind. Woe betide any newcomer, unaware of Annie's longstanding position, who tried to take her place.

Shona had spent an hour or more considering all the goods for sale on the other stalls and was making her way across to Old Annie when she saw, coming towards her, the Angus brothers. They had their arms round each others shoulders and, though it was not yet mid-day, they were both drunk.

Shona pretended not to see them and moved out of their way but Red Angus spotted her.

'I see you, Shona MacLeod!' he roared at the top of his voice.

Shona, her head down, kept on walking.

'Don't pretend. You know I'm talking to you. I haven't forgotten.'

People were turning to stare.

'I'll fix you yet! Just see if I don't!'

Black Angus was getting impatient. 'Forget her!'

'I won't forget her. She knows why!'

Black Angus pulled at his brother. 'Let's go and have another wee dram.' As he spoke he swung his brother back round to face the inn they had only just left so violently that Red stumbled and fell. When he staggered to his feet Red had forgotten Shona. He was too busy trying to persuade Black Angus to fight him to notice Shona escaping.

Just as Shona was getting close to Old Annie's pitch she realised somebody was already examining the goods. The Laird's daughter, dressed in a pink jump-suit, white high-heeled boots and a jaunty, white cowboy hat, was daintily picking over Old Annie's wares.

Shona had never been this close to Carl's sister before. She eased her way round, behind Old Annie, to get a better look at the young girl. Although she thought Donna a bit over-dressed and the boots, the heels of which had collected mud from the soft ground, were impractical, Shona had to admit she was pretty. Just like one of the princesses in the stories Uncle James loved to tell.

What shocked Shona was that this girl, who was about her age, not only wore make-up but pink pearl nail-varnish too!

Shona could not help feeling a curious pang of jealousy. A feeling she was unused to. Over the years, amongst the islanders, Shona had grown to accept her limitations but this was like peeking through a chink in a wall and finding, waiting, a totally new and different world of might-have-beens; so close and real she could smell it, but, for Shona, completely out of reach. This girl, who had everything, was so much how Shona, in her secret heart, would like to have been.

It was not her money, or her clothes which Shona coveted but her prettiness, which allowed her to give off such an air of confidence.

For a brief moment the longing and wanting bit more deeply into Shona than could any knife.

Donna was examining a pink necklace. 'How much is this?'

'Ten pounds,' Old Annie said without hesitation. Years of experience had made her a good judge of what her customers could afford in relation to what her goods were worth.

Donna obviously disagreed; she let the necklace fall back carelessly and picked up a tiny gold ring.

'Twenty pounds,' Old Annie snapped, before the girl could even ask.

'You're crazy. That isn't worth twenty pounds!'

'Maybe not,' Old Annie said slyly, 'but that's what *you'd* have to pay me before I'd let you have it!'

Donna was not used to being treated like a naughty girl, particularly by people who were usually only too glad to sell her things. Shona was amazed at how much the pretty girl's anger and disappointment, at not getting her own way, had distorted her face, all the prettiness drained away. Suddenly Donna's fancy clothes and make-up merely made her look like a spoilt little girl who had not been given the fancy dress prize.

As Donna snorted and stalked off, one heel of her boot dug so deeply into the ground that she almost fell. A passer-by automatically put out a hand to stop Donna falling but, far from being grateful, Donna snatched her arm away and limped off angrily to join her mother.

Shona, the moment of longing gone, walked round Old Annie to the front of her stall.

'What's it to be, my wee one?' Old Annie greeted her as she did every year. It paid to know her regulars. 'I've a lovely silver and emerald brooch that would look fine in your bonnet, dearie.'

Shona gazed in wonder at the glittering array of treasure which winked and sparkled in the sunlight where it lay, piled untidily on the black bag that had been spread out wide on the ground. Behind it Old Annie sat, stiffly cross-legged, her one good, brown eye watching out for the light-fingered.

There were gold rings, some plain and others encrusted with stones which might have been rubies or emeralds; fancy brooches in silver, gold or copper; ear-rings and hat pins finished off with decorated ends. There were charm bracelets, some with little animals hanging from them and others with tiny gold or silver coins which Uncle James used to say were really doubloons.

'What takes your fancy, my pretty? Something to catch your young man's eye?'

Shona laughed.

Old Annie always talked this way to her and Shona never minded. Some said she was a sooth-sayer who could see beyond the obvious, others that she was a healer (she did have charms for sale), and most knew that she was a good saleswoman with a better than average line of patter.

Amongst the shiny objects there was one that suddenly caught and held Shona's eye. It was a brooch cast in what looked like silver.

The bright oval setting was made up of intertwined sea-creatures, sea-serpents, fish and dolphins all leaping around in their silver sea. But what really attracted Shona to it was the curious large, round, dark green stone in its centre. At least she thought it was a stone until she picked it up, then a shaft of sunlight pierced it and Shona held it up to her eye.

'That's only glass, dearie, you don't want that.'

But Shona did. There were whirls and bubbles within the green glass which reminded her of looking through the piece of flawed glass that she had lost. She kept it to her eye as she turned it up to look at the green sky and then down again at the grass which it turned black.

'It's a brooch not a telescope!' Annie laughed so hard it brought on a fit of coughing.

But Shona was too busy peering through the glass, watching the curious effects the faults created, to hear. Old Annie's face was stretched sideways and downwards until she took on the appearance of a frog. The dreary white-washed inn was transformed into an emerald green under-water palace.

Shona knew she had to have the brooch. She dug deep into her pocket and held a shaking, rattling handful of coins out towards the old woman.

Old Annie sighed. 'I've prettier things than that for a young girl, but if that's what you want. . .' Her claw of a hand reached out and she picked out rather less coins than the brooch was worth. She had a soft spot for Shona and anyway, because the girl was a regular, she could always overcharge her next year! 'Will I wrap it for you?' Shona shook her head. 'Well, let me pin it on you, so you won't be losing it.'

'I – wan – ta.' Shona could not explain that she wanted to carry it and Old Annie, misunderstanding, had snatched back the brooch and was already pinning it firmly to Shona's jersey.

Shona knew that she would have a hard job organising her fingers sufficiently to open the pin again and she did so want to look through it again. Shona simply smiled and nodded at the old woman.

'See you next year, dearie,' Annie said, 'if I'm spared and you don't elope!'

The old woman's cackling laugh still in her ears, Shona set off to find her mother to try and persuade her to undo the fastening of the brooch.

'Hi, Shona!'

Shona looked up and realised she had almost knocked into Carl. Having promised herself that the next time they met she would ignore him, to pay him back for deserting her, when she looked into his blue eyes and saw his broad, even smile she knew that she could not do that. She just wished that they could have met somewhere more private where the whole island would not know about it. She felt as if everyone must be looking at them and gossiping about her being seen with the Laird's son. Shona was used to feeling embarrassed but never as badly as this. Her cheeks felt bright red.

She shifted uneasily then nodded and gave Carl one of her lop-sided grins.

'Hey, I'm sorry I haven't been around lately but I've been busy. Dad's had a whole heap of computer gear put in and I've been working with it.'

Shona did not know what 'computer gear' was – all she understood was that it had taken Carl away from her and that he preferred it to her company. She looked at the ground so that he would not be able to see how upset she was.

'Why don't you come round and see it?' Carl suggested.

Shona looked up but quickly shook her head.

Carl, thinking that he understood some of her awkwardness about coming up to the Big House, added, 'It's in the coach house round the back.'

Shona was about to answer when they were interrupted.

'Carl, your mother's getting cold, we're going to eat lunch in the car.' Howard noticed the awkward looking MacLeod girl and although he felt he ought to say something he could think of nothing until he noticed the large brooch she was wearing. 'Hey, nice brooch. It's. . .' Howard's mind raced trying to find the appropriate word, '. . .unusual.'

Shona nodded and, seeing an opportunity to get it unfastened, plucked at it with her hand, trying to show what she wanted done.

Howard did not understand the mime and was embarrassed that he had started something he could not finish. 'Yeah, I said,' he spoke louder and more slowly, as if she were deaf. 'Nice brooch! Come on, Carl, we got to eat.'

'See you at the coach house, Shona,' Carl said as he followed his father.

Shona watched them making their way through the crowd to the white Range Rover wondering if she would be able to summon up the courage to accept Carl's invitation.

The eagles had enjoyed the freedom of the island for most of the day. With almost everyone busy at the Fair down at the south end of the island the eagles had visited places they might normally avoid.

The weaker eaglet, having totally recovered from its

misadventure, had joined in with all the flying, though it had paid more attention to landing, particularly at the nest.

There had even been a chance for them to practise a little hunting. Rabbits, brought out by the quiet and the sunshine to graze on the juicy grass, had provided useful experience and in pursuing them the eagles had strayed far from their home territory.

As the afternoon wore on the wind died away completely, mist began to gather, the cloud base got lower and they were forced to turn home, flying lower than the adults would prefer.

The young ones had started to tire as the lower slopes of the Black Mountain, its top lost in a blanket of cloud, loomed up through the mist.

Through the murk the male eagle spotted a man wandering round, checking his sheep and lambs, but paid him little attention, certainly not enough to notice he carried a double-barrelled shotgun. The young eaglets were tiring rapidly and the parent birds were keen to get them safely back to the nest.

Suddenly the peace was ripped apart by a loud bang and a violent rush of air. Amongst the group of eagles there was an explosion of feathers.

One of the eaglets fell out of the sky. The male eagle instinctively accelerated, jinking right and left, the other two copied him without question. There was a second explosion but this time they were clear of the rush of air. Within seconds they were out of range of the man's gun.

The three remaining eagles flew steadily for home. The two parent birds and the weaker eaglet had survived.

'Lot 301,' the auctioneer called out to the dwindling crowd.

It was getting late, a thick, damp mist was drifting in off the sea and everyone was anxious to be either in the warmth of the inn or on their way home. Many people, including Old Annie, had already packed up and begun the long walk up the road for the ferry.

Shona was still anxiously waiting, though she could

hardly bear to watch, to see what Morag's fate would be.

'Lot 301,' the auctioneer called again, reading with difficulty from his rain-blotched list. 'What am I bid for this young Highland bullock. . .'

He broke off as everyone burst out laughing.

'You'll need to get your glasses seen to!' shouted a wag.

The auctioneer peered over his spectacles at Morag standing forlornly in the centre of the ring. He glared at his clerk but the clerk pointed at the label which did indeed say '301'.

Instantly they both knew what had happened. The children had struck again with one of their regular pranks. Hardly a Fair Day went by when the children did not swap over the labels between different animals, bringing the entire auction to a confused halt.

'So it's a cow!' the auctioneer snarled, having lost his sense of humour with his voice some hours back. 'Who's the owner?' the auctioneer demanded of his clerk. The thin, worried-looking man riffled through his clip-board of papers, the only written record of the sale which he kept inside a polythene bag to protect it from the wet, and then shrugged.

'Is the owner present?' the auctioneer demanded.

'I am that.' Mr MacLeod pushed his way to the front.

'What am I bid?' snapped the auctioneer. 'House-cow, good milker?'

But nobody was listening, they were too busy laughing and there was not a single bid.

As Mr MacLeod led Morag back out of the ring Sandy slid in beside Shona and whispered in her ear, 'Don't tell Dad. I swapped the labels round. I didn't want her sold either!'

Shona was so relieved. Morag would be going home with them for another year. The old cow, realising that at least one member of the family was pleased to see her, rubbed her face fondly against Shona's arm.

Mr MacLeod slipped the rope from around the cow's neck. Only animals which had been bought were led to their new homes, the rest were released to find their own way back. 'She'll not be long finding her way home,' Mr MacLeod complained. 'Nobody else would be so foolish as to feed her, that's for certain.'

# Fifteen

Shona woke suddenly from an uneasy sleep. A grey light was creeping round the edges of her curtains though it was still the early hours of the morning.

The family had got back very late from Fair Day. There had been a long ceilidh afterwards. Shona always loved the music. Although there was music on the radio it was not the same to her as when she could *feel* the vibrations through the soles of her feet in the room. The stories in the songs, some of the travellers were especially good at those, she particularly loved.

She would have liked to have been able to dance, the way she used to with Uncle James. He would hold her tight in his arms, her feet far from the floor, and move in time to the music so that she might experience the thrill and speed of it all as she twirled round the room, her hair flying out behind her.

Her father had tried to do it with her but he had never been a good dancer and lacked the sense of rhythm Uncle James had. But she still loved watching, the girls in their pretty dresses and most of the men, red-faced, anxious to impress, trying to look as if they were enjoying themselves.

During the last part of the walk home through the mist, with the fog-horn blaring out, Mr MacLeod had carried Shona in his arms, where she had fallen into a contented sleep.

The next thing she remembered was her mother slipping the covers of her bed over her.

'Noraag?' Shona asked sleepily. She was worried that the cow, confused by the events of the day and the thick mist, would not be able to find her way home.

'She's not back yet,' her mother said quietly. Shona moved as if to get up but her mother eased her back down again and stroked Shona's forehead. 'Now, don't you fret about Morag. She'll find her way back without anyone's help, especially when she wants milking! You get your sleep.'

Shona had drifted back to sleep remembering how many people had admired her new brooch. Even the Laird had said how unusual it was, though she did not know if Carl liked it: he had not said anything.

Now that she was wide awake, even though she might only have slept for a couple of hours, she did not feel at all tired.

Her first thought was for the brooch. Unfortunately it was still pinned to the jersey. Shona sat on the bed trying to organise her fingers to open the pin. Though the pin was not very strong Annie had gathered up so much material to make sure that it was safe Shona could not manage it. Just when she thought she had it undone it slipped back into place again.

She was still concerned about Morag and every time the fog-horn went she kept mistaking it for her mooing.

But then she heard a sound that she was certain must be Morag.

She leapt off the bed and tried to dress as quickly as possible but as usual, all fingers and thumbs, it took ages so that by the time she was outside the back door there was no sign of Morag.

The thick, damp mist swirled around Shona. Water dripped off the end of the byre on to a big, blue plastic sack. Shona could not help feeling sorry for poor old Morag wandering around in this weather instead of being warm and cosy in her byre.

Then she heard the sound again, a little way off but she was almost certain it was Morag. Maybe she needed help, had got herself entangled in some barbed wire and was bleeding to death.

Pulling on her wellingtons she set off in the direction of the sound. She thought it seemed to be coming from the main road. It was possible that Morag had followed the road and then either missed the turning off it to her own home or been prevented from reaching it by some fence or other.

The trouble was there was no more sound from Morag, if that was who it was, for Shona to follow and as she plodded through the mist she began to wonder if she was on a fool's errand.

She laughed at herself. That's me, she thought, a fool on a fool's errand!

Apart from the distant, regular booming of the fog-horn it was a very silent morning. No bird-song, not even a cockerel crowing to welcome the day. Shona wondered if she might be the only human moving on the island. The MacLeods were far from the last to leave the celebrations last night. Most people would be glad of a lie-in this morning.

Shona had been walking about half an hour with not a sound from Morag. The mist, if anything, was getting thicker and she was about to turn back for home when she thought she heard a noise like a deep cough.

She was not the only person up after all!

An amazing and frightening apparition suddenly burst through the mist. It had the head and antlers of a stag but the body of a man and it was coming straight for her.

Shona fell behind a rock like a puppet whose strings have been cut. She knew well the stories of Kings of the Forest who often took this form and who had tremendous powers over all forms of life and she was terrified that it would see her. She lay quivering with fear behind the rock, listening to the footsteps getting closer and closer.

The Kings of the Forest, half men, half deer, had been known to rescue people benighted in the forests only to keep them prisoner as their slaves. Very few had ever been seen again and those who did escape, years later, returned to their families mere shadows of their former selves.

Their intense hatred of humans came from the way men had, over the centuries, destroyed thousands of acres of forest and for this reason they could be seen not only in existing forests but on any land where trees had stood.

Shona could feel the vibrations through the earth as its footsteps came closer and closer. If she stayed exactly where she was it would see her. Even if it walked past her. They were known to have the astonishing sense of smell associated with deer. Fortunately today there was no wind to carry her scent towards it.

What she had to do was to stay hidden behind the rock and move slowly, silently round it, keeping it between them, as the beast passed.

She could hear its snorting breathing quite distinctly and began to edge carefully round the rock keeping her face and body tightly pressed against the rough surface. If only her movements were not so clumsy. She only had to make the slightest sound, dislodge a stone, to be discovered and then she would be captured.

But the beast was the one who fell.

There was a crash as the massive body hit the ground and then a curse, which Shona could not believe came from a supernatural being. She even thought she recognised the voice.

'You clumsy great fool!'

'It was your fault, you pushed me!'

It was the Angus brothers, up to their old tricks again!

'Get up and get it back on your shoulders! And make haste, there'll be people about soon.'

'I told you this was a stupid idea.'

So this was what she had heard them plotting that night up by the Big House!

Shona heard the sound of muffled grunts and curses as the men hoisted the heavy stag back up on to their shoulders. She had a hard job stopping herself giggling for believing that these two might have been a King of the Forest!

146

But the relief that she felt knowing that she was in no danger of spending the rest of her life imprisoned by a woodland beast was short-lived when she became aware of the new and very real danger she would be in if the Angus brothers discovered that she had seen them carrying off one of the Laird's stags.

Shona decided to abandon the search for Morag, she would be safer at home. She gave the Angus brothers a clear start before she began to follow. It was not difficult to follow the two men. Although she could not see them ahead of her through the mist and only occasionally heard them, there was a clear trail of dark, red blood from the dead deer.

As the brothers were obviously going home, and to do that they had to pass the MacLeod croft, all Shona had to do was follow the trail and, as long as they did not get lost, she would be home without even having to think about it.

As long as she kept her distance, rested when they did and moved when they did, it was so easy that she stopped concentrating on what she was doing and began to think of other things. Perhaps later she might summon up all her courage and go on up to the Big House, if that was the only way to see Carl again.

She was so busy with her thoughts that she did not notice the loose stone. Her foot slipped off it and she fell sprawling on the ground, sliding several feet on her front until she came to a painful stop against a small rock.

'What was that?' a voice just ahead of her whispered.

Shona lay very still, conscious of the grazes on her hands but not daring to make the slightest move to look at them. She had not realised because of the weight they were carrying how slowly they were travelling. Judging by the closeness of their voices she had almost caught them up.

'I didn't hear nothing.'

'Well, I did!'

'Och, you! You're always hearing things. The amount of drink you put away it's a wonder you aren't seeing them too!'

'Do you want to carry this beast home by yourself?'

'Don't be so daft! You know I can't.'

'You'd be in a fine mess if I left you here with it and Henderson or the Factor found you.'

'Are you forgetting the money we'll get for the venison?'

'We'll need to get it off the island first and if this mist stays down who's to say the ferry will run? Have you thought of that?'

'Let's get the damned thing home before somebody sees us. We'll worry about that all in good time.'

Shona heard them hoisting the beast up again and setting off. This time she left a good long gap before she scrambled up to her feet and made any attempt to follow.

She had been right. The trail led her safely home without further mishap and when she got back, to her enormous delight, Morag was waiting patiently just outside the fence. Shona was so pleased to see her that all the other events of the morning disappeared from her mind.

Shona was too busy rubbing her face in Morag's damp, shaggy coat to notice the shadowy figure of Henderson, the gamekeeper responsible for the Laird's deer, standing by the outer fence. Nor did she notice that the blue plastic sack had gone.

He too had followed the trail of blood and he was standing looking thoughtfully at the MacLeod croft, holding in the palm of his hand a silver brooch with an unusual green centre.

# Sixteen

Shona heard the Range Rover start up. She flattened herself against the wall seconds before it swept out of the courtyard through the big double gates – the Laird at the wheel with MacPherson sitting beside him – to be swallowed up by the mist.

Uncertain if she had been seen or not she decided it would be sensible to wait a while in case somebody had come down to the courtyard to wave the Laird off. Only when she was absolutely certain that the coast was clear did she slip as quietly as possible into the courtyard.

Once inside the gates she was amazed at the tremendous change in the old place. The weeds were gone from the gravel and the paintwork of the house was fresh and bright. There were colourful, new curtains up at all the windows.

Shona nearly jumped out of her skin when the clock above the coach house struck the half hour. Shona had never before known that clock to work.

Surrounded by mist the whole place, despite looking spick and span, had the air of rising up out of a dream and back into reality. It was no longer the eerie, deserted house it had been throughout her childhood but the lived-in bustling home of the Laird's family. Even the doors of the coach house had been replaced by huge, varnished, pine ones with solid brass handles.

Although Carl had said she should come Shona felt very uncomfortable. For the first time in her life she actually had an invitation to visit the Big House but that did not prevent her glancing back over her shoulder to see if anybody was watching, though everything around the house seemed quiet.

She put her hand on the huge, cold door handle, turned it and slipped cautiously inside.

'Mom!' Donna said as she rushed into her mother's bedroom. 'That weird kid is hanging round the place now!'

Beverly looked up from the letter she was writing. 'What weird child?'

'The one we saw on the road yesterday. The one Carl waved to. The one he said he went bird-watching with. I just saw her going across the courtyard into the coach house.'

'Perhaps Carl asked her to come. I think it's nice he has friends. It's a pity you haven't made any while you've been here.'

'My friends are all back home, having a marvellous time while I'm stuck here.' Donna suddenly looked shocked. 'You don't think he'll ask her into the house, do you?'

Beverly shook her head. 'I shouldn't think so, honey, not after yesterday.' She looked thoughtful for a moment. 'You know, there was something about the way he spoke about her then which made me think he wasn't telling us everything about that girl.'

'They're all spooky.'

'All who?'

'The people on this island. There was an old witch at the Fair yesterday who wouldn't let me buy any of her cruddy old jewellery.'

'Donna, you're imagining things. Find something to do.'

'I have.'

'What's that?'

'I'm going to wash my hair.'

As Donna left the room Beverly said, half to herself, 'Yeah, that's real exciting, don't overdo it!'

'Isn't it fantastic?' Carl stepped back, his eyes shining with excitement at all the wonderful, new hi-tech machinery his father had had installed.

He had spent nearly an hour showing Shona round. Shona had not understood one word of his explanations. She could not fail to be impressed by the smooth modern lines of the screens and keyboards but being unable to understand their real purpose made it all seem meaningless.

As far as Shona was concerned if being amongst all this baffling machinery meant that she spent time with Carl then she would endure it. Even if his explanations made her head ache and she would far rather have been out on the beach or seeing how the divers were getting along.

'I'm doing a design project over here,' Carl said, pulling up two typist's chairs, one for himself and one for Shona, and switching on one of the computers.

Instantly the screen glowed green, reminding Shona of her brooch. Instinctively she put her hand to her jersey and then realised it was no longer there!

What could have happened to it? She pulled open her coat, though she could hardly have been mistaken as to where the brooch had been pinned.

Carl looked up from his confident tapping on the keys. 'What's up, Shona?'

Shona shook her head trying to convince him that she was all right but really she was trying to think back to where the brooch could be. The last time she remembered having it was at home in her room when she was struggling to undo it. Perhaps she had loosened the catch without realising and it had dropped off later, but where?

Without thinking she stretched out a hand and accidentally touched one of the keyboards.

Instantly strange symbols came up on the screen next to the one which Carl was using to produce his complicated and colourful graphics outline.

Carl glanced round. 'Oh, that's just a word processor,' he said dismissing it as of no particular interest because he was so used to using it. 'Hey, look at this!'

He keyed in some numbers and suddenly the shape outlined in red on the screen rolled over so that they were now looking at it from the opposite side.

'See – it's three dimensional. Now I'm going to use the mouse to add to the design.'

Shona knew perfectly well what a mouse was but she could not understand what possible use one could be to Carl and anyway she saw no sign of one. Carl was simply moving a bit of plastic around.

'Isn't that amazing!' Carl said but Shona had not been paying attention, she was more concerned about her brooch.

While thinking her hands doodled around on the keyboard of the word processor. She was not aware of what she was doing, indeed as so often happened when she was not concentrating the fingers had just moved off into movements of their own.

Suddenly she looked up at the screen and saw:

ajfwp[emfw/[]] 3–9 ropq323o4 pjf.sm.fse
qo230 -1084nqp;asdv ½o358nb547[opi3
qowu 02 103784g 1/32k41%&£$!"£H!E!
zzzzzzzzzzzzzzzzzzzzzzzzzzzzzzzzzzzzzz

Shona jumped back so violently that she almost fell off her chair and Carl glanced up.

'Hey, not bad!' Carl grinned. Then an amazing thought crossed his mind. He pressed the delete key and Shona watched in astonishment as the letters and figures of her accidental doodle disappeared as if they were being eaten by some unseen mouth. Or maybe the mouse had eaten them!

'Now this is how you do your name.' Carl took hold of Shona's finger and tapped lightly on each key as he said the letters. 'S-H-O-N-A.'

Shona looked at the screen and saw her name on it. She had seen her name before. Miss Ferguson had written it up on the school blackboard.

But this was different. Tapping keys on a machine so that her name appeared somewhere else had an air of witchcraft about it that made Shona feel uneasy. It was as if she herself was being transported. Shona shuddered when she remembered how easily the machine had eaten her doodle.

Carl was too excited to notice Shona's hesitation about this discovery, he could see a whole world opening up for Shona.

'And this is how you do my name. C-A-R-L.'

Somehow seeing their two names up there side by side made Shona feel a little happier. After all if Carl was not afraid of the machine, why should she be?

'Why don't you try on your own?' Carl suggested.

Shona was not sure that she could, it was very difficult to control her fingers. Sometimes when she tried to pick a daisy she crushed the flower into a pulp. She did not want to hurt the machine.

'Try it, for me,' Carl begged. Knowing the capability of the machine he was beside himself with excitement at the possibilities for Shona if she could use it.

Put like that, how could she refuse? Concentrating fiercely she stretched out her hand towards the keyboard.

It looked baffling. None of the letters on the keys were in the right order. Shona knew the alphabet. She had sat, silently, through hours of the other children endlessly repeating it in the schoolroom. She even knew Happy Harry and all the other characters of the frieze which ran round the wall. But instead of the letters being in order they were jumbled up anyhow.

'QWERTYUIOP' ran the first line.

'ASDFGHJKL' the next.

At least amongst them she had found four of the letters of her name and the 'N' was on the bottom row.

She aimed for the 'S', trying as she did to point one finger and keep the others out of the way.

Her fingers all missed the letters completely. Instead they fell in a sprawling tangle on some keys at the end marked f1, f2, f3 and f4 and the machine bleeped in protest.

Shona jumped back as if bitten.

'It's OK,' Carl said. 'Try again.'

Shona did try but although she hit the letters this time her fingers came down in a cluster and instead of S she got:

aecw

It was no use. She had not got the control to do it. She hit her hand on the table in frustration. She so much wanted to please Carl but he was asking the impossible of her and she did not care one way or the other whether she ever managed to work his stupid machine. What use was it anyway?

But Carl was not going to give up so easily. 'Here, try doing it with a pencil. Grip the pencil in your hand.'

Shona shook her head.

'You can do it! Remember how you gripped that stone and threw it to stop me going into the quicksand?'

But that was different, thought Shona, for a start it was bigger and the need was more urgent.

'Please, just try. I know you can do it.' He offered her a red pencil, which had a rubber on the end, with the point towards her.

Desperate to please him she tried to grasp the pencil but it kept slipping out of her hand. She remembered doing the same kind of thing so many times before in school when she wished that she could write or draw like the other children. Even when the pencil had stayed in her hand the resulting scribble was so disappointing that she had eventually given up.

But Carl would not let her give up. He seemed to have an amazing amount of patience and, what was more important, he was the first person outside her own family, apart from Dr MacGregor and Miss Ferguson, who managed not to smile when she failed.

At last, by tucking the pencil point up the sleeve of her jersey he managed to get it to stay in place but when Shona tried to press down the key for S with it there was not enough strength to make the key go down. Instead the pencil just folded back towards her. There were just too many actions for her to think about. She could not possibly make all the muscles necessary to perform the act react at the same time.

Carl heaved a sigh. Shona hated disappointing him but it seemed his idea was hopeless.

'I've got it!' He grabbed a rubber band. 'Put this round the fingers that you don't need. Let me help.'

Carl gently folded all her fingers of her right hand down towards her palm except for her index finger which he left sticking straight out.

Only when it was finished did it strike Carl that Shona might find having her hand bound up like this very undignified and he looked up into her eyes. 'You don't mind, do you?'

She had tried so many things with her mother, when she was little, that she was well-used to experiments to test the limits of her abilities and if he had ever – God forbid! – seen her trying to get into a pair of jeans he would know that this was child's play by comparison. Shona shook her head.

'OK. Now try.'

Shona slowly extended her arm over the keyboard but she was still having trouble aiming it. It swung back and forth so violently that she was afraid to strike any of the keys.

Angrily she grabbed her wrist with her free hand. It worked. The extra support from the other hand acted like a tripod; it was even better when she rested her elbows on the bench beside the keyboard.

Slowly she brought her finger down and tapped S.

'You've got it!' Carl shouted.

But Shona was not listening. She was concentrating as she never had in her life before. H-O-N-A.

Carl could not believe that his idea might work. 'That's fantastic! I can't believe it. Now all I have to do is teach you how to spell and you can talk. I mean not spoken words but you could write down what you wanted to say.'

Shona was still baffled by his thinking. How could she possibly go around with a keyboard and a TV screen for the rest of her life? Perhaps she would have to walk round with them on a dinner wagon like the one her posh Aunt Effie had, perhaps Carl was mad.

'I'll teach you how to spell some other words. . .'

But Shona's fingers were hovering above the keys again. Slowly she found the letters and pressed them.

Carl looked at the screen.

It said, 'no need'.

Carl could not understand this. Instead of speaking he reached across and typed the words.

'You mean you can spell?'

'yes,' Shona wrote, 'I lurnt at scool.'

What nobody had realised, simply because there was no way for Shona to tell them, was that she had stored up an amazing amount of knowledge. Because she had no method of writing reminders for herself she had been fortunate enough to develop a very good memory. Whilst some of the knowledge, like her spelling, was a little rusty from total lack of practice, her brain was a very full store cupboard.

Carl could only sit back in his chair. Now he was the one completely lost for words. After all these years he had accidentally turned on the tap which would allow Shona's knowledge to flow out.

But Shona was typing again. It took her a long time, what with trying to find the letters and pushing them down one by one, but she made it in the end.

'Can we go for a work now,' the screen said.

Carl could not make sense of that. 'Go for a *work*?' he asked.

Shona released her wrist and used her free fingers to mime the legs of a person walking, one who staggered as much as she did, across the top of the bench.

'Oh, you mean *walk*!' And he deleted her spelling mistake and typed it in correctly.

Shona nodded and then pressed the delete key herself to remove everything from the screen except their two names. 'Shona' and 'Carl'. It might only have been superstition but she could not bring herself to let those two words be eaten.

# Seventeen

Henderson was on the main road when he saw the Laird's Range Rover loom up out of the mist and he was so anxious to stop it that he almost succeeded in getting himself run over.

'What the devil do you think you're doing?' demanded MacPherson.

'I'm sorry to stop you like that,' Henderson apologised, 'but I was anxious to have a word with you. There's been somebody after the deer!'

'What's that you say?' Howard was leaning across from behind the wheel trying to catch the conversation.

'Henderson says somebody's been after the deer,' MacPherson explained and then opened the rear door for Henderson. 'You'd best get in and tell the Laird yourself.'

'Did they get anything?' Howard said coming straight to the point.

'I think so.'

Howard was not satisfied by the answer. 'You *think* so? You're supposed to know.'

Henderson, a thin, wiry man with a weather-beaten face and sharp grey eyes, gestured at the mist that surrounded the vehicle. 'In this weather it is a little difficult to see what a man is doing even if you're standing next to him!'

Howard nodded. 'I take your point. I suppose the real question is, how come you were out there in the first place?'

'There was some loose talk down at the Fair about the deer so I made it my business to leave quietly before most people and stayed up through the night watching. It seemed the most likely time for an intending poacher to chance his arm, when they thought everyone else would still be enjoying the festivities, or at home in bed recovering.'

MacPherson nodded his approval. 'Good man! And?'

'I got well up with the herd, though not close enough for them to get wind of me and frighten them off. Then nothing all night, not until the early hours. There was just the one shot, close-by where I was hidden. Two young hinds ran past me and I found a pool of blood where a deer must have fallen but whoever killed it had made away with the body by then.'

'Or they didn't kill it, merely winged it,' suggested MacPherson.

Henderson shook his head. 'I think not. You see there was a steady trail of blood leading away from the spot, as if somebody was carrying off the body.'

Howard was showing interest again. 'Did you follow this trail?'

Henderson nodded slowly. 'Yes, sir. I did.'

'Well?'

'It brought me down here and across the road then it ran out at that wee croft over there. You can just glimpse it through the mist.'

Howard peered out through the gloom at the white-washed cottage, so consumed by the mist that the painted door and the windows looked as if they were hung in mid-air. 'Whose place is that?'

Henderson and MacPherson glanced briefly at each other. MacPherson answered. 'The MacLeods',' he muttered grimly.

'Oh, dear,' said Howard. 'Are you certain they took it?'

Henderson shook his head. 'Not certain. So far I've followed the trail to their fence and I've also been round on the other side to see if the trail went beyond. I had half thought it might have been somebody going past, but there's no sign of blood going away from the MacLeod croft. I did not want to set foot on their land without somebody with me.'

MacPherson agreed. 'Quite right.'

Howard thoughtfully rubbed his chin with his hand. 'You don't seem to have much to go on, Henderson.'

'There is something else.' He put his hand into the pocket of his oilskin and pulled out the silver brooch. 'I found this, further back, in the grass beside the trail of blood.'

Howard took the brooch with its ornate frame of silver fish from Henderson's outstretched palm and examined it closely. 'I know this brooch, it's pretty unusual and I doubt there's another like it. The MacLeod girl was wearing it at the Fair.'

MacPherson drew himself up. 'I think we should go and have a look round the MacLeod place, don't you?'

Henderson nodded his agreement but Howard looked less certain. 'I still don't think a trail of blood and a girl's brooch are enough to make out a federal case.'

'Excuse me?' said the baffled MacPherson.

'I don't think,' explained Howard, 'that on their own they're sufficient evidence on which to accuse a man of poaching.'

'Nor me,' said MacPherson, 'but I think a routine inspection for repair work would be in order.'

'With the gamekeeper and the Laird in attendance? Isn't that like sending in the heavy mob?'

'If MacLeod had nothing to hide then he might think it odd but he shouldn't take it amiss. But if he has been up to no good, well, we'll soon know.'

'I guess you're right.' Howard reluctantly started up the engine and drove down to the turning which led to the MacLeod croft. He was not looking forward to this one little bit and would have been far happier if MacPherson and Henderson were handling it alone.

As he pulled up outside the croft Howard could not help wondering if he, a man capable of running a multi-million dollar company, was cut out to run a small island. Big business was cold and impersonal. It was possible to bankrupt a man you had never met without a qualm, if only because you knew he would not hesitate to do the same to you, but these people were different. Most of them were struggling to make some sort of a living by sheer hard, physical work in dreadful conditions and helping each other whenever they could.

Also, Howard knew that he remained a foreigner amongst them, but far from feeling saddened by that fact he felt it was a privilege to be amongst them. He was anxious to have the islanders' acceptance, he would not have bought the island unless he believed he could help them, and he could not see how he could have that acceptance if he was forced to punish one of their number, even if it was for the theft of one of his deer.

When Shona and Carl had left the coach house they went for a walk along the beach behind the Big House but it was cold and damp and there was little for them to see.

Shona was disappointed. She had been longing for the kind of exploration they had enjoyed before Carl got so engrossed in his computers. Even a visit to see how the divers were getting on would have been better than nothing but Carl would not have noticed even if a purple gryphon had walked along the sand towards them, he was so busy talking about the word processor and how useful it would be for her.

What Carl did not seem to understand was that the machine was no help to her out here! She could not answer his questions on the beach, nor could she stumble back to the coach house every time she had something to say!

As they tired of being blotting paper for the mist Carl tried to persuade her to go back to the coach house but Shona's head was beginning to ache with all his talk and she did not want to spend all her time with him pushing buttons on a keyboard.

Shona shook her head, pointed towards her home and he agreed to let her go on the understanding that they would meet up at the coach house the following day.

As she drew close to home the first thing she saw was the Laird's Range Rover parked outside. Guiltily she wondered if he had somehow found out that she had been, with Carl, using the precious machinery in the coach house and had come to complain. But that was not possible! She had seen the Laird leave and he certainly had not returned before she had left with Carl.

Why else would he come?

As she came round the corner of the house she saw the Laird, her mother and her two brothers standing uncomfortably silent in the misty drizzle and at that moment MacPherson came out with Henderson and her father. All three looked very upset. MacPherson was carrying by its hoof the leg of a dead animal.

Shona's first thought was that it must belong to Morag, but that was impossible. Although it was a similar colour it was far too thin to be from a cow. Then she realised it was from a deer. But how could that have got into their byre?

Then a picture came into her mind, from earlier that morning, of the Angus brothers, struggling through the mist with the dead stag slung over their shoulders. She also remembered the threats Red Angus had shouted at her, about getting even, not only with her, but with the whole MacLeod family!

Instantly everything dropped into place for Shona. The plot she had overheard them making that night up by the Big House, the threats and the deer they had killed were all part of the same horrible scheme, to make a dishonest profit out of the Laird whilst, as a bonus, getting their own back on the MacLeod family.

'I keep telling you, I've never seen that before in my life,' her father was saying, through teeth clenched in anger. 'I was as shocked to find it there as you were.'

'Which doesn't explain how it got there,' MacPherson snapped.

'Obviously somebody put it there,' Mr MacLeod muttered under his breath.

'But who? That is the relevant question.' MacPherson drew himself up and went on, pompously, 'I hope that you are not suggesting that either of us . . .'

'I wouldn't put it past you,' Mr MacLeod shouted. 'You're anxious enough to get us off that land of yours so that your precious deer have more grazing. You'd stop at nothing to avoid having to renew my agreement.'

'That's outrageous!' stammered MacPherson.

'So is accusing me of poaching. I've never taken a thing that did not belong to me in my whole life.'

Henderson avoided their eyes and cleared his throat uncomfortably before he spoke. 'Unless we can find some satisfactory explanation for the presence of that haunch of venison in your byre then we have to be forgiven for assuming the obvious, MacLeod.'

Mr MacLeod sharply drew breath and was about to reply when he thought better of it. He was clearly in deep trouble, anything he said could only make matters worse.

While the three men had been arguing Shona had moved unnoticed to her father's side. Shona hated arguments and this one could so easily be stopped, she knew all the answers.

Shona plucked at her father's arm to attract his attention but he shook her off, as if she had been an irritating fly.

'Apart from the time I was out at the Fair, for all to see, I've been with my family. You can ask them.'

'Oh, yes,' Mr MacPherson nodded knowingly, 'and they would say what we would expect them to say. What kind of alibi is that?'

Shona tried again to intervene before matters went any further. Frantically she pulled at the sleeve of her father's jacket but he shrugged it out of her grasp and rounded on her.

'Not now, Shona. Run away and play. Can't you see that I'm busy?'

Tears of hurt sprang into her eyes. He had never spoken so sharply to her in her entire life.

She would show them! 'I – warra – ellu – goth,' she shouted. The words corkscrewed out of her mouth in a wild torrent before Shona lapsed into silence.

Two of the three men, MacPherson and her father, stared

at her, while Henderson stirred round the mud of the yard with the toe of his boot.

Henderson recovered first. Taking his hand from his pocket he held out the brooch Shona had bought from Old Annie.

Shona, delighted that her lost brooch had been found, reached out to take but Henderson's hand snapped shut like a clam.

'I found this beside the trail of blood which led back to this house,' Henderson said grimly.

'You surely aren't suggesting that my daughter is capable of killing a deer and carrying it back here!'

'No,' MacPherson cut in. 'But she could have been with you. You said earlier that apart from when you were at the Fair the whole family were with you, the only disagreement would seem to be over exactly where you were.'

Shona's mother, who had stood, grim-faced, her arms folded, spoke for the first time. 'You have known my husband ever since you've been on this island, Mr MacPherson, and you know as well as anyone that he is an honest, straightforward man in his dealings with you and everybody else.'

'Mrs MacLeod, I understand what you're saying but, faced with the evidence, what other conclusions can we draw?'

'Then,' Mrs MacLeod drew herself up, 'it's my belief there's nothing more to be said. I wish you good day!'

She flapped her arms at the boys, driving them towards the house like hens, then putting her hand on Shona's shoulder she withdrew from the scene leaving her husband to see the visitors off the premises.

Shona, knowing that she carried the key to all this unhappiness, tried hard, when they were back in the warm comfort of the living room, to talk to her mother, to unravel the mystery.

She stroked her mother's arm and tried to form the words of explanation but Shona was far too agitated, so they would not come and her mother, for once, did not help her.

'Not now, Shona, I am too upset just now.'

She stirred the peats under the kettle and as a column of thin, black smoke trickled up the chimney the boys, also affected by the tension in the air, broke into a mock fight.

'If you want to behave like that, get off to your own rooms and do it. I won't have it in here! Now, be off, all of you and leave me in peace!'

Shona did not want to be alone but in this mood she knew her mother must be obeyed so, while the boys went for a rough and tumble, Shona stood silently by her window looking out at the grey mist, wondering what she could do.

It was when she heard the Laird's car pulling away from the house and Shona began thinking of Carl that the solution suddenly came to her.

Carl's processor, or whatever he called it!

Even if she could not say the words, using that thing she would be able to write them down!

There was no time to be lost. The longer she waited the greater the opportunity for the Angus brothers to dispose of the evidence of their crime.

She had to go back to the Big House and hope that Carl was still in the coach house.

Then she sank back down on to the bed. Why should they believe her? Simply telling them was not enough. It would be just her word against theirs. The Laird's men had found evidence, undoubtedly carefully put there by the Angus brothers where it could easily be found, and if they were to believe her she must find some.

The thought of going anywhere near their broken-down old cottage filled her with terror but Shona knew she had no choice if she wanted to prove her father's innocence.

Opening the door of her room she could hear the muffled, serious voices of her parents deep in conversation in the living room and her brothers' raucous shouts still spilled out from behind the closed door of their bedroom.

Slowly, so as to make no noise, Shona slipped out of the house by the back door and disappeared into the mist.

The nearer Shona got to the Angus brothers' cottage the

louder grew the noise of the fog-horn. For once she took comfort from its plaintive bleats, welcoming them as familiar sounds in what she thought of as frightening surroundings.

This was one of the few parts of the island that she never normally visited, like most islanders she knew that it was best avoided.

She was even grateful for the thickening mist, for the finger of land where their cottage stood offered little cover. The tall dunes dropped away to become only occasional clumps of spiky marram grass leaving the cottage sticking up like a single rotten tooth from a mouthful of pale gums.

In front of the cottage the remains of a small rowing boat were propped up against a low stone wall. The boat had been reduced to a skeleton as the brothers had cannibalised it for the few, slipshod repairs they had ever carried out on the cottage.

To avoid being seen from the inside Shona crept cautiously down the side of the cottage on her hands and knees, though as most of the broken windows were filled with damp cardboard that danger was reduced. As she crouched down behind the low wall raised voices drifted out through the door which hung open on its broken hinges.

'I told you from the beginning it was a daft and dangerous idea.'

'It would have been all right but for the mist.'

'Last night you said the mist would give us good cover. You can't have it both ways!'

'I wasn't to know it would thicken so much that the ferry wouldn't run, was I?'

'And now we can't get the damned venison to the mainland to sell it. It only needs the Factor to come nosing round and we'll both end up in jail.'

'The Factor won't come down here looking. That trail of blood we left leading to the MacLeods' and the haunch of venison in the byre were enough to put him off the scent.'

'We've still got to get rid of the thing. I don't feel safe with it lying around the place. You never know who might see it.'

'Nobody ever comes here.'

'It's going, I tell you.'

'You can please yourself.'

'And you're helping. On your feet!'

There was the scrape of a chair leg on bare floor tiles and a clatter as it fell over. 'Watch what you're doing.'

'Get hold of the end of this beast and let's get the thing outside before the mist lifts and everyone can see what we're doing.'

'It'll not lift tonight.'

'All the same!'

Shona heard grunts and heavy, staggering footsteps coming towards the door. It was easy to tell they had had time to celebrate the success of their plan with a few drams of their favourite drink.

Shona kept her head well down until she heard them go past the end of the wall. Where were they taking it? Surely they could not be carrying the rest of the carcass back to her home? They would never risk that in daylight while her father was about!

'You've forgotten the spade!'

They were going to bury it!

'I didn't forget the spade, you did!'

'It was you that wanted it out of the house, no me!'

As Black Angus staggered drunkenly back for the spade Shona ducked down so quickly that she dislodged a piece of loose stone from the wall. It rattled down the spar of the old boat.

'What was that?' snapped Black.

In the silence which followed the fog-horn bleated its lonely call. It sounded more than ever like a calf calling for its mother.

'What was what? I heard nothing but the fog-horn.'

'I did. There's somebody around the house.'

Red laughed. 'You're starting to imagine things now,' he scoffed. 'Your brain is addled with the drink. It'll be pink elephants you'll be seeing next.'

'I tell you I heard something.'

Shona held her breath and pressed herself tightly against the rough, damp stones of the wall, knowing that should Black Angus happen to glance over it he could not help but see her.

'Get the spade and let's get on with the job, if we must!'

Black Angus collected the spade, to Shona's amazement, from the living room and rejoined his brother. Together, grunting and grumbling, they hoisted up the carcass of the beast and carried it off round the back of the house.

It was not difficult to follow them. The tip of the dead stag's horns had dragged a V-shaped groove in the soft sand as they carried the heavy body.

Shona shivered as she peered round the corner of the cottage at the macabre sight of two wild looking, unkempt men, their hot, whiskied breath billowing out into the mist, as they stooped over what looked like a grave for the dead creature which lay on the ground beside them, its huge, terrified eyes gazing up in the frozen stare of death.

Beside it, on the ground was a bloodstained, blue plastic sack, the very one she had noticed outside the byre at home. So that was how they had managed to make the trail of blood stop at their croft. When the Angus brothers had hacked off the leg to leave behind to incriminate the MacLeod family they must have stuffed the end of the animal's bleeding body into the sack.

'It needs to be deeper than that,' Black said impatiently to his brother as they paused in the digging. 'We don't want some stray dog coming along and digging it up.'

At last the hole was deep enough to satisfy both of them. The animal was lowered into it and the sand piled back on top.

'You can see that's been freshly dug,' Black protested.

'The sand will soon dry out.'

Black shook his head. 'That's not good enough. Scatter some dried sand over the hole and then we'll put some driftwood over it.'

Once they had finished putting on the dried sand Shona thought their work was so convincing that she was not certain that she would be able to remember well enough where the animal was buried to tell anyone but fortunately the brothers marked the burial place with some lumps of driftwood. One of these, a lump of tree root blackened and worn by the shifting seas until it had taken on the look of a goat's head, clearly identified the spot.

Shona had seen enough. She slunk off, back along the beach, into the mists before the brothers returned from their work.

Perhaps she should tell her parents what she had seen, but she realised that apart from the difficulty of getting her story across that way, it would be far better if the Factor were present when the body was discovered. If her father told the Factor about finding the buried animal the Laird could say that her father had put it there in order to divert suspicion.

No, tired as she was she had to finish the job she had started.

The journey back along the beach was long and slow. She was cold, wet and hungry. She hadn't eaten since breakfast and she wished that she had brought some food with her, even a bar of chocolate. She no longer knew whether it was morning or afternoon. So much had been crammed into the day since she first woke that it seemed to have been unrolling endlessly, like pulling the loose thread of a jumper and having the whole thing unravel in a shapeless pile at her feet.

Shona was feeling doubly guilty as she climbed the dunes at the back of the House because in amongst all the troubles the thing which concerned her most was the loss of her brooch. Mr Henderson might at least have returned it but she supposed he must be keeping it as evidence.

There was a sense of loss about it that mystified her until she began to picture in her mind the ornate, silver frame with all the shapes of fishes and sea-creatures worked into it and then she suddenly realised why it had appealed so much to her. It was all because of Uncle James. It reminded her of all the stories he told about those things and the life he used to lead on the island.

If only he had been here now, none of this would have been happening, he would have known how to make it all better!

But there was no time for day-dreaming. The solution was in her head and the sooner she got it out the better!

By the time she reached the Big House the light, muffled by the mist, was draining out of the day. Shona could see lights in several windows behind drawn curtains. Shona stopped. When she had left home there had been no doubts in her mind, not only that she would find Carl in the coach house but that she would be able to write out the words with the help of his machine which would explain everything, but now she did not feel nearly so certain.

She felt cold and lonely, wished only to be back in the warmth of her own home. But then, realising there would be little comfort for her there either if she failed in what she had set out to do, indeed they might soon lose their home altogether, she forced herself to continue.

The courtyard was silent. Nobody in the house seemed to be stirring.

Cautiously she set out, hugging the wall yet being forced to negotiate the noisy, scrunching, loose gravel whose echoes came back from the walls of the high, silent house.

But when at last she reached the coach house door it was only to discover that it was locked!

As Shona was wondering what to do next the sash of an upstairs window slid open with a protesting squeal, a shaft of light trapped her in its glare and a girl's voice pierced the silence of the yard.

'Hey, you! What do you think you're doing?'

Shona searched the back of the house until she found a curious, pale apparition in a white turban peering down at her through the mist.

For a split second Shona believed she had seen a ghost but surely no ghost on this island would have an American accent?

'Clear off, why don't you? Stop hanging around here.'

Shona was frozen by the shock of discovery.

'What's the matter, honey, you shouldn't be near that open window when you've just washed your hair.' A second face appeared at the window. It was the Laird's wife.

'It's that weird girl again.' Donna pointed an accusing finger at Shona who stood, arms akimbo, her back against the coach house door.

'Shut the window, I'll get your father!'

The sharp slam of the window more than the words she had just heard galvanised Shona into action. She had seen enough of the Laird for one day. Having accused her father of poaching one of his deer he would probably now accuse her of an awful crime if he caught her.

Slipping and scrambling over the loose gravel, her heart pounding, she left the courtyard, was through the gate and hidden, breathless, amongst the trees beside the house by the time she heard the back door bang open.

'But she's perfectly harmless,' Carl protested to his father. Having heard who was the cause of all the fuss he had come running out into the yard with his father.

'I don't care about that. For one thing she frightens your sister . . .'

'Donna's frightened of her own shadow,' Carl interposed scornfully.

'That's enough! It isn't just that. The MacLeod family are involved in poaching and we're going to have to turn them off some land. The whole deal is very unpleasant to say the least! The less we see of the MacLeod family for the time being the better. So don't encourage her to come up here any more. Understand?'

'Yes, sir!'

Both angry in their separate ways they turned back towards the house, Carl anxiously looking over his shoulder wondering where Shona was hiding.

Shona felt betrayed. When she first heard the back door bang open Shona had expected that Carl would come running after her to tell her that everything was all right, it was all a misunderstanding. That of course she could come into the coach house and use the machinery to tell the true story of who had killed the Laird's deer.

But how could he? He did not know the reason for her visit. By now Carl had probably heard the Laird's version of events and believed that the whole MacLeod family were thieves. After all, had not one of the MacLeods assaulted him, knocked him to the ground?

Shona could hardly blame him but she still felt that he had deserted her and it hurt! She had not hesitated to help him. She thought they were supposed to be friends!

Under the shadow of the huge stone which formed the gatepost Shona sat hunched on the ground, her cold tired limbs aching, as she watched and waited, like a trapped animal.

# Eighteen

'Shona must be somewhere!' Mrs MacLeod protested. 'Have you looked in the byre?'

All four of them stood in the yard behind the cottage, their clothes dripping, their wet hair plastered tight to their skulls, their anxious faces lit only by the yellow light from the hurricane lamp Mr MacLeod carried. He nodded. 'I've searched everywhere I can think of.'

'And we went down to the beach,' Sandy said.

Andrew, next to him, added, 'We went almost down to the Angus brothers' and up to the quicksand and we called all the way.'

Mrs MacLeod shook her head. 'She's gone off before, but never like this!'

'Wait until I get her back,' Mr MacLeod muttered grimly. 'I'll give her a piece of my mind!'

'That's the trouble!' His wife turned her fear into anger and directed it all at him. 'I know you've problems enough at the moment but you were hard on the girl this morning.'

'Aye, that's right, blame me for everything.'

Mrs MacLeod sighed. 'You're not to blame any more than the rest of us. We all take far too much for granted as far as Shona's concerned. I suppose we'd best go in and eat. There's nothing more we can do out here. But if she's not back in an hour we'll have to get help.'

'An hour?' Mr MacLeod's face was drained by worry. 'It'll be pitch dark by then and in this fog we'll see nothing. I'll go up the road a piece and see what I can see.'

'Andy and I'll come with you, Dad,' Sandy volunteered.

Mr MacLeod shook his head quickly. 'You stay here.' Then he added, avoiding their troubled eyes, 'You never know what help your mother might need.'

Shona woke with a start as the coach house door slammed. She was stiff in every joint and her back ached from being pressed against the cold stone of the gatepost. Carl and his father were standing in a pool of light which made the damp stones of the courtyard glisten.

'Carl, you left the lights on.'

'I know, I'm coming back after supper to finish up. You needn't bother locking up.'

The Laird peered suspiciously through the mist. 'I feel uncomfortable leaving everything open, but if you say.'

Shona thought she saw Carl look directly at her as he turned towards the house with his father. Maybe she had imagined it or had he been expecting her to return ever since his father had sent her away? He might even creep out of the house to meet her. At the very least he should be able to make it safe for her. In an emergency he could always manage to get out first and warn her if anyone was coming.

Feeling a little safer, Shona hauled herself up. Her right leg had developed pins and needles, from being curled up beneath her, so that as soon as she put some weight on it it almost collapsed.

At last, the feeling rubbed back into her leg and all quiet at the house, she crept into the yard keeping in the shadow of the wall for as long as possible.

When she reached the coach house she ducked awkwardly under the lit windows so as not to run the risk of being seen, no matter how briefly, in silhouette. When she touched the handle she half expected alarm bells to ring out but there was no sound beyond the drip, drip, drip of moisture off the buildings.

Once inside there was so much light Shona felt as exposed as a goldfish in a tank, but there was no time to waste. She went straight to the machine she had been using with Carl.

What if it was not switched on? Suddenly she remembered he had had to push all kinds of switches before it was ready for her to use. But again she was in luck and she felt more than ever convinced that Carl had been expecting her to return. The screen glowed slightly and the little rectangle of white, which showed where you were up to, winked mechanically at her.

Throughout the day she had carried with her the image of her fingers flying over the keys, rather as she had seen Carl's when he operated the machines, but the reality for Shona was very different.

Her fingers blue with cold were even worse than usual. She could not straighten them out and they appeared to have no strength in them at all. Whenever she managed to touch a key the finger crumpled under the slightest pressure until it was the knuckle which came down on the key two rows above the one she had been aiming at.

Shona's dream of how she would write her story had certainly not included the minor indignity of binding her hand with the rubber band. Now it seemed she would not only have to use that but she would have to strap a pencil into the contraption to replace her useless fingers.

Putting the band on to her own hand was no easy task. Carl had made it look so simple, just a flick of his nimble hands and the band was in place. For Shona, trying to get the band round her fingers without it flirting away across the room seemed as possible as wrapping the sun in a parcel.

After several frustrating failures it suddenly appeared to flick into place almost of its own accord. One minute it was hung round the finger of her left hand like a small, dead eel, the next it had wrapped itself neatly round her right hand, binding down all but the index finger. But the finger curled so limply that Shona had to find a pencil and force that in under her palm into the hole formed by her folded fingers.

That worked no better than her own limp finger. The pencil's hard, shiny end, she had put it in point first, slid off the keys and hit others instead. Added to which, the pencil sticking out at right angles to her hand meant she had to work sideways which was even more awkward.

Shona was keenly aware of time running out! Either she had to get it right soon or she would have to leave. After all, there was no guarantee that Carl would be the first person to return to the coach house.

Eventually she turned the pencil round, hooking the point through her curled up thumb, so that it acted as a splint for the finger she wanted to use and gave it just enough support.

Shona glanced up at the screen. At the top was a line of errors from her earlier experiments:

'a 9 0 =]½ pppppppppp'

Shona had forgotten the existence of the key which she had thought of as eating words and this was no time to be fussy. There was not a second to be lost if she was to get her story down.

Slowly, painstakingly but with a complete absence of punctuation and wild guesses at words she had only previously heard spoken and never seen written down her finger moved laboriously over the keys.

Even her left hand, which gripped her right round the wrist to help guide it, grew tired but still she carried on. Her eyes wanted to drift off to sleep in the warmth of the coach house, having been out in the cold for so much of the day, but she forced them to look at the keys and then up at the screen to check the sense of what she was writing.

It was an hour later that she got up from the desk and staggered off into the night leaving a garbled but crucially important message on the screen to be read by the next person who looked at it.

Carl had not hurried over his meal. In fact he had not seen Shona lurking in the shadows although he had been looking out for her, had been expecting her to return all day. He knew there was something wrong with the story his father had come home with about Shona's father poaching deer. Carl could not persuade himself that Shona, who loved birds and animals so much and seemed to know so much about their haunts and habits, could possibly have a father who would go out and shoot a deer, especially one that did not belong to him.

Even having been thumped by her brother did not convince Carl that the MacLeods were violent people now that he had come to realise that the boy had only done what he had to protect his sister's feelings.

His own sister had no such doubts.

'I'm not a bit surprised,' Donna said towards the end of the meal. 'If the father didn't kill the poor deer I expect that awful girl put the evil eye on it!'

Carl had not bothered to stay and hear his mother's rebuke. He had left the table and walked straight out to the coach house.

Eagerly he went over to the desk and saw the message Shona had left for him.

At first sight Carl was disappointed. It looked as if what she had left was gobbledegook but when he looked more closely he realised that hidden amongst the mistakes and misspellings there *was* a message. He swiftly pressed the buttons which set the chattering printer in motion so that he could show his father a copy.

'Dad!' he shouted as he burst into the room. 'Look what I just found on the word processor. Shona must have been up here while we were eating.'

Howard looked angry. 'That girl! I told her to stay away and I told you we should lock up.' Then a puzzled look crossed his face. 'How come she can use a word processor? From everything I've heard the kid's hardly been educated.'

'I'll explain it all later, but read this!'

Howard looked at the sheet of paper and shook his head. 'I can't make head nor tail of any of it.'

Carl shrugged. 'It's easy. I'll read it to you.'

And as he read it out loud he pointed to the words on the page.

'6deercarlwasw notkilled8 bi mii dad
itwasthee anaangusbruthers2 weniwentto

thehowstoday tha wurhidingthebodi
be hindthehows in thesand undur a
   gotes head
      shona'

Howard's face was a picture. 'A goat's head? You mean they killed a goat too?'

Carl grinned. 'I guess so if that's what she says. All I know is, we'd better get down there soon before the Angus brothers decide to dig the deer up and make off with it.'

His father looked doubtful. 'Oh, come on, Carl! We've only got this kid's word for it. Could be a wild-goose chase.'

Carl was serious. 'Dad! You said yourself you were surprised MacLeod was involved. Now Shona's offered you the proof.'

'We don't know it's *proof*,' his father pointed out. 'The girl could be lying.'

Carl looked very steadily at his father. 'She might possibly lie to you, but no way would she ever lie to me. That girl saved my life.' There, it was out and Carl felt better for having said it.

His father stood up. 'It seems to me you've got a good deal of explaining to do but we'll discuss that in more detail another time. Where is she now? Still out in the coach house?'

Carl shook his head. 'No, there was no sign of her. I guess she took off in case you turned up again.'

'I'll ring MacPherson, have him pick up Henderson and we'll see what's going on.'

'Thanks, Dad.'

# Nineteen

As the ferry pulled away from the quay to be swallowed up by the darkness, the only person to watch it go was Mr MacPherson. Even while the lights were still disappearing into the night mist he climbed back into the white Range Rover and sat for a second rubbing his hand possessively over its substantial steering wheel, so different from his old mini. He could not help thinking how lucky he was once again to be free to enjoy the comfort and luxury of the Laird's car now that they had all gone.

Driving off he could not help thinking how surprised the islanders would be when they heard the news. The island was still buzzing with the arrest of the Angus brothers. This would really give them something to talk about!

It had come as quite a surprise to MacPherson too.

They had been sitting in the office finalising the draft for the renewal of the MacLeod land lease, at a lower rent, when the phone rang. Carl had answered it but quickly handed it across to his father. 'Dad, it's a hospital in Chicago for you, they say it's urgent.'

Mr Kleinberger said little as he listened to the voice at the other end but his face became grimmer by the second. Eventually he snapped out, 'We'll be there just as soon as possible.' He slammed down the phone. 'Carl, tell your mother to pack, we're leaving.' Carl gaped at his father who had already turned away to MacPherson. 'When's the next ferry?'

MacPherson checked his watch. 'In an hour's time.'

'I'll need you to drive us down.' MacPherson nodded but found it difficult to conceal his amazement.

'Dad, what's the matter?'

'It's your grandmother. She's had a heart attack. They found her in her apartment. Nobody knows how long she'd been like that. I knew we shouldn't have left her on her own. Go tell your mother to be ready to leave in just under an hour.'

'Are we all going?'

Howard looked shocked. 'Of course. They say she only stands a fifty-fifty chance of pulling through. Now go tell your mother while I raise the London office and get them to fix a flight schedule and some tickets.'

Only Carl and his father stood at the rail watching the tiny lights of the island slipping away into the darkness.

Donna and her mother were in the relative comfort and warmth of the State cabin. They had no regrets about their departure. Donna was delighted that her father's personal jet would be waiting at Glasgow airport to speed them even quicker to Chicago.

But there was a question Carl had not dared to put into words until now.

'We are coming back, aren't we?'

Howard shrugged. 'I don't know, son. Your grandmother is in a pretty bad way. Even *if* she pulls through, she's going to need a whole lot of nursing. I don't know if I could risk us living thousands of miles away from her again like this.'

'I guess Mom and Donna will be pleased anyway.' Carl felt his mouth go dry as a frightening possibility crossed his mind. 'You won't sell the island, will you?'

'Why, son, would you mind?' Carl's mind was too full to allow himself to speak; he nodded vigorously. Howard smiled at him. 'You've managed to settle in better than any of us, I guess. In fact you've had a great time, haven't you?'

Carl thought through his exploration of the island and his

friendship with Shona and all the wild animals and birds they had watched together and realised, probably for the first time, just how special it had all been. It was something that he would never forget for the rest of his life. All the days he remembered were sunny, the murky, misty ones had evaporated.

Howard only remembered the mistakes he had made, particularly over MacLeod and the deer. Despite apologising to MacLeod and trying to make it up to him Howard knew that, although the man might eventually forgive him, he would certainly never forget being falsely accused of poaching the Laird's deer.

That made Howard feel more of an intruder than he had ever felt since he had come to the island and it had made him reconsider all his plans for its future. Not that he had discussed his feelings with anybody, that was not his style, but it made him wonder how much of a bulldozer he was in his attitudes to other people.

Howard rubbed his big chin in the palm of his hand. 'I can't help wondering if I've been of any help to the islanders. Most of the projects I had in mind are still in the pipeline.' He shrugged. 'Maybe change isn't what they need, maybe they're happier as they are.'

'You said, when we first came, something about being a footnote on the page of history. I think they need some help if they're going to survive but when it comes to what they need perhaps *they* should be allowed to decide,' Carl said quietly.

'Do any of us really know what's best for us?'

'I guess most of us don't,' Carl admitted, 'but in a way the islanders care more about the island than they do about themselves. Mostly they just want to keep it going, make sure it has a future.'

His father nodded. 'Shrewd thinking! I guess you're right. I ought to let them get on with it and not interfere.'

'That isn't what I said at all, Dad! Sure they need help and you can put ideas to them that are from outside their experience, after all you've got your finger on the pulse of the world's business. But in the end they ought to be allowed to figure it out for themselves. Plan for the future without destroying the past, or the present.'

Howard grinned. 'Hey, kid, you're turning into quite a business visionary.' Carl blushed. Howard looked thoughtfully at his son for a moment before he spoke again. There was something new about the boy. In spite of natural fatherly pride he'd always thought of him as something of a nerd but the way he'd stuck up for the MacLeods, that was new. 'How would you like to take on the job of running the island?'

Carl's breath was taken away by the marvellous, frightening possibilities of this suggestion. 'I'm not up to that, Dad!' he gasped.

'Not right away, but one day you will be and until then you could help out on it. After all I've got a hundred and one other things to take care of. I don't want to sell the island, there are still tax problems connected with that, but I could set up a trust for the islanders with me as head until you're old enough to run it yourself. How does that grab you?'

'All right!' Carl's eyes flashed with excitement and pleasure at the thought of being able to return to the island. Happily he stuffed his hands deep into the pocket of his anorak and then the expression on his face turned to one of alarm.

He had forgotten to give MacPherson his letter for Shona.

'She won't eat, Doctor, and she hasn't even got out of bed today,' Mrs MacLeod said. 'It's not like Shona at all. She's never had what you'd call a day's illness in her life. I just don't understand.'

Dr MacGregor's eyes flashed over his half-framed spectacles. 'I'll take a look at her.'

Mrs MacLeod bustled across the tiny kitchen to show him through but Dr MacGregor held up his hand. 'I know the way, thank you, Mrs MacLeod, and I fancy I would manage this best on my own.'

He pushed open the door of Shona's room. She was lying

on her bed, her face buried in the pillow. She did not stir when he closed the door behind him.

'Well, young Shona, it seems you are worrying your mother half to death. What's the problem?'

Shona did not move.

'I'd best take a look at you. Turn over.'

Shona hesitated for a moment before she awkwardly rolled over. Although he was too experienced to show it, Dr MacGregor was quite shocked at how pale and drawn she looked compared to when he had last seen her. Her eyes were pink-rimmed, as if she had been crying.

He noticed that while he went through the routine of checking pulse and temperature she avoided meeting his gaze. Even while he was checking her chest with his stethoscope she managed to keep her eyes focused on the bedroom wall.

Finally he put away his instruments and sat on the bed beside her.

'Shona, there's not a thing wrong with you. Why won't you get up?'

She did not reply but her eyes instantly filled with tears, one of which rolled slowly down her cheek. She did not brush it away. It splashed on to the sheet leaving a dark, damp patch. Shona's face was the picture of misery.

Dr MacGregor cleared his throat. Normally he was a brusque man, unaffected by tears, but he was not insensitive and knew the difference between crocodile tears and the genuine article. Besides which, he knew that Shona, who had more reason than most, was not one to give in easily. Gently he took hold of her hand. 'Come on. It can't be that bad. What's bothering you? You know you can tell me anything.'

Shona shook her head. She made no sound but several more tears dropped and widened the dark pool on the sheet.

He waited several minutes but there was obviously going to be no response of any kind. With a sigh he heaved himself up off the bed. 'I'll look in and see you again tomorrow, Shona. I'd like to see you up and about by then. You're not ill and I'm sure that whatever it is that's bothering you can be solved if you'd only let us know what it is. In the meantime I'd be grateful if you didn't worry your mother into an early grave!'

Shona sat perfectly still as the Doctor left the room, her face hidden by her long, tousled hair, looking down at the tear-stained sheet.

'I can't make her out, Mrs MacLeod. There's nothing medically the matter with her, I'm almost certain, but she's dreadfully unhappy about something. If I didn't know her better I'd say she was pining for something.'

Mrs MacLeod shook her head. 'It beats me! I would have thought she couldn't have been happier. Her father was so relieved when the matter of the deer was cleared up and that was all Shona's doing.'

'Yes, I heard about that. She wrote it all down I heard. That was truly astonishing but isn't it what we've always said? We knew there was a key if only we could find it to unlock what was stored away inside the child.'

'Not with a pencil, you understand, with some kind of machine up at the Laird's house.' She paused for a moment looking puzzled. 'How she got in there I'll never know.'

'Mmm!' the Doctor said thoughtfully.

'But fancy Shona being able to write at all! She never showed the slightest inclination at school or at home.'

'But it was all going in at school, she was storing it all away in her mind. It's what I've always said about her,' he said proudly, 'you never know what's going on in her mind.'

'Particularly at the moment,' Mrs MacLeod said, shaking her head. 'I should be up at the peat cuttings with the rest of them. Thinking we might have to leave we hadn't bothered so we're all behind. Instead I'm stuck here nursing a sick child who isn't really sick!'

'Be patient, Mrs MacLeod. Give her until tomorrow. She may not be sick but something has bitterly upset her and we must find out what it is.'

Shona gazed bleakly at the wall. Just when she had thought

everything was going to be perfect it had all fallen apart.

When the Laird had visited the house, apologised to her father for wrongly accusing him of poaching, told him that the Angus brothers had been caught, and that not only would the MacLeods be able to stay but the extra land, essential for the grazing, was to be theirs again, she had felt so happy that she thought she would burst. The Laird had even thanked Shona for her part in solving the mystery, congratulated her on her use of the word processor and returned the silver brooch.

But when MacPherson had next day brought round the contract for the land and happened to mention, in passing, that the Laird and his family had left unexpectedly, with no plans to return, Shona felt that the end of the world had come and her precious brooch lay unheeded on the dressing table.

There had been so many things that she had been dreading. The first had been having to go to the mainland school and the next was possibly having to leave the island for ever in disgrace. But Carl leaving the island, never to return, was worse than all of those and something she had never even considered.

What made it worse was that he had not even bothered to come and tell her. Their friendship clearly meant so little to him that he had just packed his bags and gone.

Shona rolled over and hugged her damp pillow for comfort.

It was two days later when Fergus the Post pulled up at the door in his red van.

'Not more bills, is it?' Mr MacLeod called, as he emerged from stacking peats beside the house.

'Not a bit of it,' said Fergus. 'It's a letter from America.'

'I expect it's from my brother James.'

Fergus, who recognised the handwriting of everyone who wrote regularly to the island and was well known for handing letters over with words like 'It's from your cousin in London', shook his head. 'Not a bit of it,' and then added knowingly, 'It's postmarked Chicago.'

'Let's have a look at it then,' Mr MacLeod said, holding out his hand. He had an awful feeling in the pit of his stomach. He knew as well as everyone that Chicago was where the Laird had gone and he could not help thinking that this letter was from the Laird to tell him that he had changed his mind about the grazing land.

Fergus clasped the letter secretively to his chest. 'It's not for you! It's for young Shona.'

'Shona?' Mr MacLeod could not believe his ears.

Fergus nodded. 'That's right. And as an official of the Post Office it is my bounden duty only to hand over the Royal Mails to whom they are addressed.' Fergus, who had never before delivered a letter for Shona, was clearly enjoying this moment of power!

Mr MacLeod called towards the house. Shona had got dressed but had eaten no breakfast, spending her time either moping around the house or sitting on the sofa under the window gazing out uninterestedly at the landscape. Even her brothers' teasing had failed to move her and at last they had given up and gone out to play on the beach.

She reluctantly appeared in the doorway.

As Fergus marched up to her, his waders flapping round his thighs, his hand went up to his Post Office cap in a salute and he handed over the letter. 'For you, Miss MacLeod, from America!'

Shona looked at the envelope with its foreign-looking stamps but joined-up writing defeated her completely and the only bit she could read was the 'Air Mail' sticker.

'Will I read it to you?' Mr MacLeod asked.

Without answering Shona took the letter and turned back into the house leaving the two men deflated, shuffling their feet and wishing each other good day.

Dr MacGregor, more worried than he would admit by Shona's behaviour, had got into the habit of calling daily on the way back from his rounds, just as he had when she was a baby. When he arrived that day she was in her room staring out of the window and the envelope lay unopened on the windowsill beside her.

'What's this then?' he said, tapping the letter with a forefinger.

Shona shrugged.

'You haven't even opened it. Shall I do it for you?' he asked, when she did not reply. Again she shrugged but she turned to look when, after the Doctor had slit open the envelope and pulled out the flimsy sheet of paper, a key clattered out on to the sill.

Her hand clumsily grabbed the key and held on to it tightly; this was no flower and she could not damage it.

The Doctor offered her the letter. 'Aren't you going to read it?'

Shona looked at it blankly.

Dr macGregor was surprised. 'I heard you could read. So why won't you read this?'

Shona simply shook her head. How could she explain the difference between capital letters on the school blackboard or the word processor and these joined-up ones which, in black ink, made the paper look as if it were covered in spider's webs?

Dr MacGregor glanced down at the end of the letter. 'It's from Carl. The Laird's son, Carl, you remember?' He was astonished at the difference this information made. She snatched the letter out of his hand, almost tearing the flimsy airmail notepaper in her eagerness to touch something that Carl had once touched.

Her eyes feverishly scanned the writing on the page but she could understand little more than the address at the top which Carl had printed out in block capitals. Frustrated her fist closed, crumpling the letter.

'What does it say, Shona?' She turned her head away. 'Don't you like the letter?'

Shona began to sob but she did not throw the letter away, instead she pressed its rough edges against her cheek, a gesture Dr MacGregor had come to recognise as one of affection.

So that's it, he thought. Carl was the reason for her being so upset these last few days. Somehow they must have met

186

and formed some kind of friendship. He did not know how but these days nothing surprised him, especially if it concerned Shona. Now she was upset because he had left the island.

But if that was true why had his letter upset her so much? Even if it reminded her of Carl's absence he would have expected her to be pleased to receive a letter from him.

He knew he would never properly understand the workings of the female mind! It was not totally by accident that Dr MacGregor had remained a bachelor!

'Shona, won't you even let me see what the letter says?'

Reluctantly she passed the crumpled ball of paper to him. He carefully pressed it straight on the windowsill and read silently to himself.

The sight of this almost drove Shona demented. She grabbed the Doctor's arm and frantically shook it, at the same time pointing at her mouth.

'What on earth is the matter, Shona? Are you hungry?' he asked, misunderstanding her mime.

She shook her head and pointed at the letter then at the Doctor's mouth. Her hand went back and forth between the two and then she wailed, 'Weed! Weed!'

'You want me to read it?' Shona nodded. 'I'm sorry, I thought you'd already read it.' He cleared his throat and began to read the words from the page.

'Dear Shona,

I'm sorry that we had to rush away the way we did but my grandmother was taken very sick in Chicago. As a matter of fact they thought she was going to die but she is through the worst of it now and starting to make a good recovery, although she is still paralysed down her right side and has great difficulty talking.

I hope you won't mind me saying this, but knowing you has helped me to understand a great deal better the problems she faces. When I look at her it's very hard sometimes to remember that inside she's still the lively, kind person she always was and that the stroke has affected her body but not her mind. So I talk to her a lot, even though she can't always answer me and I've told her a lot about the island and everybody on it, especially you. Donna won't even go visit with her but I think it would be terrible for her to be locked away all on her own.

I really wanted to come and see you to explain everything about us having to leave but we only had one hour to catch the ferry and I meant to leave a note with MacPherson for you but in the rush I brought it with me instead.

Because what I most wanted to do was to leave the key to the coach house for you to use. Just because we aren't there doesn't mean you shouldn't go on with practising your writing. In fact I'm trying to find some learning programmes for you to use and I'll get them shipped over as soon as I can. Maybe then you won't have to leave the island for your education.

Give my love to the divers!

Yours,

Carl.

P.S. The equipment is all switched on so that Dad can keep in contact with MacPherson (don't know how MacPherson feels about that!), so if you get stuck ask him. I don't think he understands it but he might be able to help you!'

When the Doctor had finished reading the letter he folded it up and handed it back to Shona. 'Well, isn't that wonderful? Now you can use the coach house whenever you like.'

Shona showed no sign of understanding and although she still held the key in one hand it was the letter with which she stroked her face while the tears streamed down her face.

'I thought she would have been pleased,' Dr MacGregor said to Shona's mother as he prepared to get into his old bull-nosed Morris. 'I believe that there is a whole Aladdin's Cave of technology up there, not that I understand any of it, but which the letter says she can use.'

Mrs MacLeod sighed. 'Perhaps it is the boy she misses more than the writing,' she suggested.

The Doctor looked quite baffled by that thought. 'Oh! Do you really think so? I never thought of that.'

After the Doctor had gone Mrs MacLeod went into Shona's room. She was still standing, silent by the window. Her mother went up close and slipped an arm round her waist.

'I hear you have the run of the Laird's coach house with all that wonderful machinery.'

Shona nodded but her mother could see her eyes were still full of tears and the letter was screwed into a ball by the tightness of her fist.

'I think maybe you should go up there,' her mother suggested.

Shona let out a wail of anguish. How could she possibly go up there? It would only be a reminder of Carl. Come to that there were so many places on the island that were now reminders of the time they had spent together, which was why she had not set foot outside the door since he left.

Her mother pressed on. 'I think you *should* go. No doubt Carl would like a letter from you, to know that you are all right. Otherwise he might worry.' Shona did not move but her mother had an idea that something of what she said had struck a chord in Shona's mind. Quietly she slipped out of the room to leave her to think over what she had said.

It took Shona a long time to get to the coach house. All the way she kept telling herself she was not really going there at all but just out for a walk to get some good fresh air. But each step took her closer and eventually she found herself slipping the key into the lock and turning it.

The room was shaded from the afternoon sun and until she switched on the lights the VDU screens glowed like vacant fish tanks. Every step she had taken had, as she had expected, reminded her of Carl and had been agony for her. Now standing in the room that was so much part of him it was almost overwhelming and she wanted to turn and run away but she held her ground.

Her body was trembling with the mixed feelings of nearness to Carl, almost able to see the intense blue of his eyes and the brilliant blond hair, and yet the separation from him.

When she had at last got her feelings more under control she sat once more in front of the word processor. The one she had struggled so hard with to produce the garbled message which had saved her father from disgrace and the whole family from eviction.

Maybe it would have been better to have been evicted. Perhaps she would have been better off never seeing the island again. If Carl was not going to be there she would not be able to bear its constant reminders.

She sat before her own green screen – the modern version of her long lost piece of flawed glass. She doodled her hands across the keyboard and a line of characters appeared.

What use would a letter be anyway? How could that bring them closer together? Shona began to suspect that her mother had said that simply to get her to come up here so that she would write again, though not necessarily to Carl.

Shona was about to leave this place, so full of bitter memories, when a monitor on another desk bleeped twice sharply. It was so unexpected that the shock took Shona's breath away.

It squealed again like a tiny, hurt animal. When Shona went across to look at the monitor she could not believe her eyes.

'Hi Shona, you should have had my letter by now. If you are there all you have to do is type, just like you did on the other machine, and we can talk to each other. How are you?'

Shona thought this must be some kind of trick or magic. Carl could not possibly be sending these words thousands of miles across the sea, now, this very minute, could he? And waiting for a reply? It was so like shouting messages to Uncle James on the west wind and waiting for replies on the east ones that she could hardly bring herself to believe in it.

But as a true islander she had always had a strong belief in the impossible and in magic. Had she not, all her life, prayed for a miracle?

The machine made her jump as it bleeped again.

'Shona, are you there? Just type yes.'

Shona suddenly jerked into life. He was there! It was real!

She tried to get her fingers organised but they would not work! Frantically, while the monitor squealed its hurt at her, she searched for the rubber band to support her fingers. She found it at last but it would not go on.

The monitor's squeals seemed to grow more frantic. If she did not reply soon maybe he would give up and go away!

At last the rubber band was in place. She rushed back to the desk.

'Shona, are you there? Just type yes.

Shona, are you there? Just type yes.

Shona, are you there? Please type yes or anything.'
had appeared on the monitor.

Maybe he had given up, gone away? No, the cursor flickered across the screen trailing words behind it like a snail's trail.

'Shona, are you there? Just type.'

Shona carefully tapped out 'Y E S'. As she typed each letter it appeared on the screen but Shona still could not believe that Carl in Chicago could read them until she saw his reply.

'Shona, it is so good to hear from you. Did you get my letter?

How are you? There's so much I want to ask but first I have to say how much I'm missing the island. I can't wait to get back there. Shona, I miss you so much.

You talk now.'

Tears made it almost impossible for her to see the keys as she tapped in her message:

'deer carl i love you. . .'

ALSO IN

HEINEMANN
NEW WINDMILLS

Founding Editors: Anne and Ian Serraillier

**Chinua Achebe** Things Fall Apart
**Douglas Adams** The Hitchhiker's Guide to the Galaxy
**Vivien Alcock** The Cuckoo Sister; The Monster Garden; The Trial of Anna Cotman; A Kind of Thief
**Margaret Atwood** The Handmaid's Tale
**J G Ballard** Empire of the Sun
**Nina Bawden** The Witch's Daughter; A Handful of Thieves; Carrie's War; The Robbers; Devil by the Sea; Kept in the Dark; The Finding; Keeping Henry; Humbug
**E R Braithwaite** To Sir, With Love
**John Branfield** The Day I Shot My Dad
**F Hodgson Burnett** The Secret Garden
**Ray Bradbury** The Golden Apples of the Sun; The Illustrated Man
**Betsy Byars** The Midnight Fox; Goodbye, Chicken Little; The Pinballs
**Victor Canning** The Runaways; Flight of the Grey Goose
**Ann Coburn** Welcome to the Real World
**Hannah Cole** Bring in the Spring
**Jane Leslie Conly** Racso and the Rats of NIMH
**Robert Cormier** We All Fall Down
**Roald Dahl** Danny, The Champion of the World; The Wonderful Story of Henry Sugar; George's Marvellous Medicine; The BFG; The Witches; Boy; Going Solo; Charlie and the Chocolate Factory; Matilda
**Anita Desai** The Village by the Sea
**Charles Dickens** A Christmas Carol; Great Expectations
**Peter Dickinson** The Gift; Annerton Pit; Healer
**Berlie Doherty** Granny was a Buffer Girl
**Gerald Durrell** My Family and Other Animals
**J M Falkner** Moonfleet
**Anne Fine** The Granny Project
**Anne Frank** The Diary of Anne Frank
**Leon Garfield** Six Apprentices
**Jamila Gavin** The Wheel of Surya
**Adele Geras** Snapshots of Paradise

**Graham Greene** The Third Man and The Fallen Idol; Brighton Rock
**Thomas Hardy** The Withered Arm and Other Wessex Tales
**Rosemary Harris** Zed
**L P Hartley** The Go-Between
**Ernest Hemingway** The Old Man and the Sea; A Farewell to Arms
**Nat Hentoff** Does this School have Capital Punishment?
**Nigel Hinton** Getting Free; Buddy; Buddy's Song
**Minfong Ho** Rice Without Rain
**Anne Holm** I Am David
**Janni Howker** Badger on the Barge; Isaac Campion
**Linda Hoy** Your Friend Rebecca
**Barbara Ireson** (Editor) In a Class of Their Own
**Jennifer Johnston** Shadows on Our Skin
**Toeckey Jones** Go Well, Stay Well
**James Joyce** A Portrait of the Artist as a Young Man
**Geraldine Kaye** Comfort Herself; A Breath of Fresh Air
**Clive King** Me and My Million
**Dick King-Smith** The Sheep-Pig
**Daniel Keyes** Flowers for Algernon
**Elizabeth Laird** Red Sky in the Morning; Kiss the Dust
**D H Lawrence** The Fox and The Virgin and the Gypsy; Selected Tales
**Harper Lee** To Kill a Mockingbird
**Julius Lester** Basketball Game
**Ursula Le Guin** A Wizard of Earthsea
**C Day Lewis** The Otterbury Incident
**David Line** Run for Your Life; Screaming High
**Joan Lingard** Across the Barricades; Into Exile; The Clearance; The File on Fraulein Berg
**Penelope Lively** The Ghost of Thomas Kempe
**Jack London** The Call of the Wild; White Fang
**Bernard Mac Laverty** Cal; The Best of Bernard Mac Laverty
**Margaret Mahy** The Haunting; The Catalogue of The Universe
**Jan Mark** Do You Read Me? Eight Short Stories
**James Vance Marshall** Walkabout
**Somerset Maugham** The Kite and Other Stories
**Michael Morpurgo** Waiting for Anya; My Friend Walter; The War of Jenkins' Ear

*How many have you read?*